the Firebrand River

Nancy Smith

This book is a work of fiction. Names, characters, places and incidents are a product of the author's imagination. Any similarity to actual persons, living or dead, or events is entirely coincidental.

the Firebrand River

Author: Nancy Smith
Printed in the United States
Published 2022, by First Look Publishing (Austin)
www.nancysmithwriter.com
Version 1.0

ISBN Number:
979-8-9854983-0-1 Firebrand River (print)
979-8-9854983-1-8 Firebrand River (digital)

Cover Design: Nancy Smith
Editor: Yellow Bird Editors

Table of Contents

ACKNOWLEDGMENTS

Thank you to all my advance readers who take time to read and offer constructive comments.

Thank you to Kat Catmull at Yellow Bird Editors who provided enough compliments on both this book and *The Universal Vaccine* in order to keep me going as well as very comprehensive and helpful edits and comments. I appreciate it even when she is pointing that I keep doing the same things over and over.

Thanks to David Barnett who always offers an all-embracing proof.

Thanks once again to author Patrice Sarath who makes the writing and editing process fun.

Part I

Chapter 1 - *Mira* - March 2003

The doorbell rang in the dark and woke up four-year old Mira. Holding her doll, she shuffled down the hall from her room to her Mommy's bedroom. Mira shook her arm.

"Wake up," Mira said, but Mommy didn't.

There was a party dress on the floor and Mira knew that Mommy slept hard when she'd been to a party.

The doorbell rang again.

"Mommy. Wake up," Mira wailed.

She knew Mommy would say "no" if she opened the door herself, but she went down the hallway toward the front door anyway.

She could reach the bottom lock on her own, but she couldn't reach the top lock, so she went to her pink bathroom. Mira set down her doll on the floor and got her stool with the stickers on top. It was a little bit heavy, so she dragged it down the hall. It made a loud, scrapping noise.

She unlocked the bottom lock, and then the top one. A scary man she did not know opened the door. He was holding up her daddy. He pushed her out of the way and pulled Daddy inside.

"Your dad isn't feeling so good," he said. He struggled to get daddy into the fancy room and onto the couch that no one ever sat on. "Tell your mama to take him to the doctor in the morning. Okay. Ya hear me?"

Mira began to cry. Daddy looked bad.

"Make sure she does now."

The man took off Daddy's shoes. He touched Mira's head, and then walked out the door.

Mira turned on a light. She shook Daddy's arm. His eyes opened for a moment and then the brown part disappeared and

there was only white. Daddy's face looked blue. No matter how hard she pounded on him, he didn't wake up. He was sleeping hard too, but then, Daddy went stiff and his arms, legs and head started jumping around. Daddy fell off the sofa.
Mira screamed and screamed.

Chapter 2 - *Mira* - March 2020

Mira shepherded her dad, Carlton Ashe, to a ball game at the University of Texas Disch-Falk field. The weatherman had threatened rain that had never materialized. It was a cool, sunny afternoon.

Dad gave Mira money to buy a dog and a soda from a vendor, but he didn't want anything to eat for himself. While in line, Mira watched him progress slowly toward the gate with the aid of his walker. At the entrance to the stands, he moved the walker out of the way and waited for her. Mira joined him and helped him to climb the two steps to the hard metal seats for which he had paid a fortune as they were near the entrance, on the lowest level and on the aisle.

Mira sat down next to him and dug into her dog.

The grass in the infield was the most intense green that Mira had ever seen. It looked fake, like plastic grass, but she knew it was real because she could smell it.

Two months before her eighteenth birthday, Mira had rushed out of the house to start college, and since then she hadn't been spending heaps of time with her dad. He rarely went anywhere or did anything, so it was up to her to go to him. Today, he didn't look well and she felt guilty for dragging him out, even though it had been his idea. He'd insisted.

Dad had serious respiratory problems related to a work-place accident he said he suffered years ago. Some guy brought him home in the middle of the night unable to breathe right and having convulsions. Mira's screams finally woke her mother who called 911. No doctors, including expensive specialists, seemed able to help him. All the experts were unsure what was wrong with him.

As if to demonstrate, Dad wheezed and struggled to get comfortable in his hard seat. Mira went to his walker and got the cushion from its seat. She helped Dad up enough to put the cushion on the hard metal. She set his mobile oxygen concentrator beside him. Dad didn't like the machine, but would use it if need be. She placed her hand on his arm and left it there for a minute.

Mira was having fun living in the dorm. She liked being a college kid on her own. And she was enjoying watching the game with her dad. It was conflicting.

As the players switched at the bottom of the second inning, Mira knew that they would not make it to the end of the game. Dad looked worse than when they had arrived. The sun moved over first base and directly into their eyes. Mira had left behind her sunglasses in the car, so she lifted one arm to block the glare. The batter hit the ball out of the Disch. The crowd roared.

Her father said, "I'm not going to live much longer."

Mira went blind. She couldn't see if the hitter hit or the outfielder caught the ball. She didn't know if they continued to play the game. She couldn't be certain the sun continued to shine. She felt bile in her throat. The constant distress of being sickly had made him listless and depressed, especially in the last few years. He'd attempted suicide once before, but that was a couple years ago.

"I don't want you to hurt yourself," Mira said.

"It's not that," he said.

She wondered if she believed him. "Then what?" Dad didn't respond. He gave her a look that said, *You know.* Mira felt afraid, skeptical and confused all at the same time.

Dad wheezed for a minute, and then said, "They've done all they can. It's my time."

Mira was trying to process what he was saying. She almost didn't hear what he said next.

"I got a payout for my lungs from my employer back when it happened."

This was the first Mira had heard of that. "A payout? From whom? What employer?"

"With it, I bought a plot of land—forty acres of beautiful undeveloped hills and fields beside the Colorado River," he told her.

She didn't stir, so he went on.

"The Colorado was originally named as Rio del Tizon by Spanish explorers which translates as Firebrand River. The locals in the small town nearby use the name Firebrand on their main street and a few historic buildings, and so the river in that section has come to be called Firebrand as well. It's about eighty miles west of Austin." He choked out his next words. "It's a real doable drive."

Mira heard, but didn't know how to respond. She was in shock.

"I've left the land to you in my will. I've got a property manager, a realtor named Alonzo Rossi. Your Mom will pay him until you're finished with college and law school, if you still want to do that."

"What are the doctors saying? What can be done?" Mira asked.

"You know what they say. My lungs and heart are giving out. All my major organs."

"Maybe we can try again to find another specialist."

"Don't sell that land. Hold on to it."

Chapter 3 - *Mira* - Friday - April 24, 2026

Mira had been an twenty-one-year-old senior at the University of Texas at Austin when her father died horribly. They called it heart failure, but it was his heart, his lungs and the general lack of care he took of himself.

Her dad had always been her best person, the one with which she had the deepest relationship. That was probably because of all the time she had spent caring for his health. He'd loved her and was always there for her as best he could be, but she had felt as if she had been his caretaker most of her life–both physically and mentally. Her dad had been her man-child, silly, immature and reckless. She missed him utterly, but couldn't shake her sense of relief nor the guilt that that relief brought to her.

As he had promised, Dad left her forty acres of land in his will. Her mom had gotten the house, the car and her–although Mira no longer saw her mother. Mira was angry with Mom since the day she moved Dad into assisted living and left him there for his last year of his life. And, she'd rarely been in town to go and see him. Instead, Mom preferred to live in France and so she sold the house two months after Dad died and left Mira all alone.

After her Dad died and her Mom left, Mira had moved from the dorm to a tiny Austin studio apartment. Due to COVID-19, she was forced to isolate there for more than a year. She'd been sick with grief and didn't mind being alone as much as she thought she might. She ate junk food, took her classes online and watched television. In-person classes started again in spring of 2021, but she couldn't drag herself back to campus for in-person classes until the next fall. She spent this time studying for her Law School Admissions Test. Still in a hurry to start her life, she took her LSAT at the soonest offering after graduation and applied to law school at U.T. By then, she was utterly sick of herself and of her apartment.

The land, the only thing she had left of her father, became like her family. It was forty acres of trees, flowers and hills with the Firebrand River running along the eastern edge. It was beautiful and it had saved her sanity.

It had been her idea. She randomly invited people out to a volleyball party. Usually, around noon on Saturdays, people would gather. Everyone brought his or her own food and drinks, cooking out on an open pit grill. A few people brought tents and spent Saturday night by the river. It was a cheap way to take a mini-break and meet lots of guys doing it. She was very popular at school. Everyone wanted to get to know the girl with the land down by the river.

Law school was arduous; still, for the last few years, Mira had made the hour and a half drive from Austin to the land on Friday nights. She liked to be alone before the others came out on Saturdays. She would make a fire in the pit, study her books as well as the stars and relax.

Mira turned twenty-four last December. She would finish her classes next week; the following week, she would complete her exams, and then at the end of May, she would graduate law school with a J.D. She had less than two months left to go.

Mira listened again to the message on her phone from Alonzo Rossi who was a real estate agent as well as her property manager. Mira had seen him once at her father's online memorial, but she hadn't met Rossi in person since the reading of the will. She remembered him as a country boy, small, wiry and fidgety, in scuffed cowboy boots. There was something about him she just didn't like, and so she avoided him when at all possible.

"I got a client who is interested in purchasing your property off Highway 71," Rossi said. "If it's convenient, we'd like to stop on by the land tomorrow afternoon about two o'clock."

Mira had lost her father when he died. She lost her mother to

France. If she sold her land, she would lose everything else she had. Mira was drowning in her losses. But, she had been offered a great first job in Memphis. She planned to passed her bar exam in Texas over the summer. If she took this job, she would clerk for a year until she passed the bar exam in Tennessee. She was seriously considering it. *Maybe it's time to start over,* she thought, *build a life on my own.*

She called back and left her own message. "Two o'clock is fine." She wondered if Rossi knew she was there nearly every weekend. He worked at the same real estate office as Riley Miller so he easily could.

Mira was on edge already when a dry storm, lightning and thunder with no rain, hit, so she hadn't made her Friday night drive to the land. She sat at the window in her apartment staring out. There was something terrifying to her about a storm with no rain, so she packed up, but never left for her property.

Her phone rang and she picked up. "Hey."

"How you doing—storm and everything?" her friend Andee Wilder asked.

Mira listened to the silence in her apartment. She could hear the hum of the refrigerator—white noise that filled her mind. She glanced at the clock on her laptop computer—nine o'clock in the evening.

"You're still home?" Andee went on. "Want to meet for breakfast in the morning?"

"I bet I can guess where. Pancakes?"

"You got it."

"Ten o'clock. Be on time."

"Sure." Mira stretched out on her bed. The storm ceased its onslaught, her eyes grew heavy and eventually she fell asleep.

In the morning, Mira took a shower, put on some clothes, and puttered around a bit. She needed to get moving. Andee was always so serious. She would get upset if Mira showed up too late — although she likely expected Mira to be a little bit late.

Mira rolled her head and stretched out her arms. She felt like she couldn't put her shoulders down. They stayed scrunched up almost touching her ears.

She looked around at her tiny efficiency apartment. It wasn't a good place to have been quarantined. It was nothing more than a closet with a few sticks of furniture. She hadn't fully decorated, existing here, never really moving in. She took a bed, a glass-top desk and a big overstuffed chair from her mother's house right before her mother moved out of the country. Currently, the chair was covered in dirty clothes. Rumpled sheets and wet towels lay disheveled on the bed she had slept in since she was a child. They reminded her that she needed to do laundry. She wondered if her apartment would smell like mildew to anyone coming in from the fresh air. She sniffed, but only picked up the faint scent of bug spray.

Her desk was covered with law review manuals, notepads scribbled with her small handwriting and anything else that didn't have a place of its own. She shut down her laptop and packed her equipment into the cross-the-shoulder bag she had quilted and put together herself. She rolled her wrists which ached from hours of sitting at an undersized, non-ergonomic keyboard.

She was greeted by warm sunlight when she opened the door. A car honked its horn as it passed by on the noisy street outside. Her town life was encroaching on her country life. It used to be easy to get away for a bit on weekends. It wasn't anymore.

Chapter 4 - *Mira* – Saturday, April 25, 2026

It was spring. Everywhere, Mira's world was being refreshed. The trees were leafing out in a chartreuse color. Bountiful buds promised white and pink flowers in a matter of weeks. Bluebonnets, that were really almost purple, were popping up in random patterns in the fields and by-ways.

Workers were remodeling a little strip mall down the street from the café where she was to meet Andee. Trucks lined the easement making parking near the restaurant a problem. Mira had to go around the block twice before she found a place into which she could slide the nine-year-old, silver Chevy Volt. She parallel parked on a side street in front of a white frame house.

The owner of the house, a skinny, gray-haired woman with an oversized tummy, watched from her front porch. Her glare was wary and unfriendly as Mira left her eyesore of a car too close to the woman's territory.

"Morning," Mira called with fake cheerfulness.

The woman glowered, but did not lash out to protect.

Mira walked on, relieved that there would be no confrontation.

The sidewalk and cement steps to the restaurant entrance were lined with beds of petunias and impatiens. People loitered around the door in an informal line or sat on the steps, smoking and enjoying the warm spring day.

Mira worked her way through until she was inside. She could smell coffee and ginger pancakes. Andee waited at a table by the front window. She wore a blindingly white sleeveless top and blue jean shorts. Her long legs crossed away from the room and her gaze was to the outside. She was watching, waiting impatiently. Mira could see the worry on Andee's face.

Mira's shoes clomped loudly as she walked across the wood floor to join her friend. The server followed her to the table.

"Coffee," Mira said.

The front window was open and a light breeze carried the fragrance of the marigolds, dill, basil and peppermint from the window boxes outside.

Andee was fingering her paper napkin. Her chestnut hair was as curled tight as her demeanor. Her thin lips formed a hard line. Andee was pretty now, but if she didn't relax, she wouldn't be at forty.

Andee heard Mira's arrival and turned toward her.

Mira smiled at Andee and held her palms together under her chin, making her apologies. "So sorry."

"It's okay. You're here now. I was anxious to talk to you."

You're always anxious, Mira thought.

And then she saw him. He seemed to be staring at her, but not in an unpleasant way. Mira caught his eyes and held the look. She smiled. It was something she practiced, making eye contact and willing a man to cross the space between them. He had an attractive face, high cheekbones, a long, straight nose and a strong, square jaw.

"What are you going to eat? I might get a breakfast burrito instead of pancakes."

Andee was talking to her, but Mira was distracted. The man stood up and walked over, his heavy steps resounding on the wood floor. He had the long stride of a tall man. She guessed he was about six foot, maybe six-two.

"Do you know me? I can't believe I'm saying this. It's not a line," he said.

At close inspection, he was very impressive. He wasn't classically handsome, but had a masculine power to him. She felt drawn to him. He wore a blue tee shirt that lay smoothly across his broad shoulders and chest, and then narrowed down to lie neatly over jeans that covered his thin hips and powerful thighs.

She felt like she did know him. He seemed familiar. She felt trust and comfort, like you would with a friend from childhood. She stared into his large, steel-gray eyes. She wanted to know him, but she didn't think that she did — yet.

"No," she said. "But that can be remedied if you join us for breakfast."

Andee gave her a kick under the table and imperceptibly shook her head.

"I didn't mean that. I don't want to impose."

"Please." She listened to the sound of her own voice and wondered why she was begging him.

He nodded. "I would love to. Back in a minute." He went back to his table and picked up his cup of coffee.

"Are you crazy?" Andee asked. "He's a stranger."

"You're always the voice of caution. Half the people that come to my land every weekend are strangers. I like meeting new people."

He sat opposite her at the table. The waitperson refilled all their coffee cups and took their order.

"I just moved to Austin. I haven't met very many people yet. It's nice to have some company."

"When did you get here?"

"Feels like yesterday," he said.

"We're on our way to a volleyball party. There'll be lots of people there. Want to come?"

"Miles Lynton," he said.

She hadn't even thought to introduce herself. "Miranda Ashe, but my friends call me Mira."

"Mira." Andee had a cold look of calculated caution in her eyes.

She ignored it. "No. I'm Mira. You're Andee."

Chapter 5 - *Mira* - Saturday - April 25, 2026

Mira left her tiny electric car parked on the street in front of the angry woman's house. She waited with Andee at her car. Mira would drive with Miles to show him the way and Andee would follow them in her own car.

"One of these days, you're going to regret being so trusting," Andee said.

"I hope not," Mira responded as Miles pulled up and she got into his car.

On the drive, Mira and Miles talked about the usual "getting to know you" things. Miles asked a lot of questions and listened intently to her answers. This was one of the early tests she had when Mira met a new man—did he talk only about himself or did he want to know about her too. He passed.

"You said you just arrived in Austin. From where?" Mira asked.

"Washington," he said.

"D.C. or state?"

"D.C. Really I live more in Virginia, but I work in Washington, D.C."

"For who?"

"I work for the government." Mira had read somewhere that saying you worked *for the government* meant you worked for the FBI, NSA or CIA. She decided not to pursue it further now if he didn't. She waited, but he said no more about it. "I've been to Virginia Beach once," she said instead.

"Yes. Blue crabs. I love those."

"Your accent doesn't sound like east coast to me."

"I lived in Texas growing up—in Austin in fact," Miles said.

"Coming home, huh? Your folks live here?"

"Something like that." He looked sad. "My mother lives in Austin. I lost my father when I was a kid."

"How old were you?" Mira asked.

"Seven," Miles said.

"When my dad died, it was horrible. I was twenty-one. I can't imagine going through that at seven."

Mira let the conversation drift back to inconsequential things and the remainder of their drive flew by. Mira liked this man more and more with each thing he said. She was smitten and not just with his pretty face.

Traffic jams and construction gave way to open fields and open road. Soon, they were only a few minutes from her property.

"Would you stop here?" Mira pointed to a little grocery store that she frequented. "Sometimes I feel like I practically live at this little store on the weekends. I'm just going to pick up a few things."

He smiled at her. "I'll wait here." He opened his window to let in some fresh air and kicked back.

"You want anything?"

"No thanks." He slid the seat as far back as it would go and set one foot on the dash. She watched his long fingers brush stray blond hairs from his eyes.

The store was in a small, old house that had been converted for the purpose. The front porch was screened in. A picnic table sat under the tin roof with an antique ceiling fan blowing hot air. A couple of the local folk sat at the table drinking beer. Mira nodded a hello and the two men waved back. Andee joined her on the porch. Mira glanced back one more time before entering the store's front door. It looked like Miles was on his phone. She guessed he had plans to cancel. She wondered who with.

A small bell jingled as they opened the door.

"Hi Dottie," Mira called.

Dottie was reading the latest *Seventeen* magazine even though she hadn't seen seventeen in at least sixty years. Her waist-length hair of an unnatural orange color was pulled back into a ponytail. She was wearing a crop top that looked scary on a woman of her age.

"My favorite little chickees," Dottie called good-naturedly as Andee joined Mira.

Mira picked up a small basket and filled it with sparkling water, chicken for the grill and vegetables to make salad. On impulse, she picked up a small bag of candy. She put the items on the counter.

"All your friends buy the smallest packages I have, just enough for themselves," Dottie said. "You always buy the largest sizes."

"I like to have extra in case it's needed."

"It's always needed because you buy it."

"When are you going to come out and play volleyball with us Dottie?" Mira asked.

"When you gonna work this counter so I can?"

"We'll get Andee to stay. You don't mind, do you?"

Andee stammered, not certain what to say.

Dottie touched Andee's hand. "She's joshing you. She's joshing both of us." She handed Andee one bag of groceries. "Watch out for her." She handed Mira another.

At Miles' car, Mira put her bag into the back seat. She looked into the sack and pulled out something.

"Here," she said, tossing the bag of candy. "I have some kisses for you."

Miles lifted one eyebrow in surprise.

Chapter 6 - *Mira* - Saturday, April 25, 2026

Miles lay his hand gently on the small of Mira's back as she guided him through the crowd of regulars who had gathered by the volleyball net. Her skin warmed where he was touching her and she felt her face flush. She tried to look casual and unaffected.

"Sweetheart, I could get jealous."

Mira jerked around and saw Riley Miller and another man walking toward her. Riley was a tall man with sinewy muscles and curly hair in a trendy, lopsided cut. She hated Riley at that moment. He was always teasing, saying they were a couple, but they were absolutely not. She had met Riley in her freshmen year of college. He was one of the first people she invited out to the land, so Riley was someone she has known a long while. She liked him at his core, but she absolutely, definitely didn't want to date him or marry him.

Riley put on his real estate persona. "Miranda Ashe, I'd like you to meet Jayson Brookshire from Andover and Associates. Alonzo became suddenly ill this morning, and since I was coming out to see my best girl anyway, I offered to bring along his client."

"Mr. Brookshire." They exchanged a firm, no nonsense handshake. She noticed the skin on his hand was callused, but he had manicured nails. He wore his blond hair close-cropped on the sides and his blue eyes were made brighter by a deep tan. He looked corporate in his casual pants and crisp cotton shirt, but like maybe a boater or sailor on the weekend. He was attractive, but in his corporate clothes, he wasn't attractive to her, but in jeans and a tee-shirt, he probably would be.

"Would you excuse Mr. Miller and I for just one minute?" Mira grabbed Riley by his arm and dragged him a couple feet away. When safely out of earshot, she punched him hard on the side of the arm.

"Awah," Riley grunted. "That hurt."

"You have got to stop calling me Sweetheart and Darling and Honeypie. I am not your best girl. We are not a couple."

"But we're gonna be?"

"No." Her voice got shrill. "How many times must I say 'no'?"

His tone became solemn. "Until you say 'yes.'" He walked back over to the others.

"Mr. Brookshire," Riley started.

"Can't we get a little more casual on this beautiful Saturday afternoon." He smiled at Mira. Call me Jayson," he said.

"Jayson," Riley picked right up. "Mira and I are ready to show you around the property."

"Jimmy Rey," Mira called out to a friend of hers who was standing close by. "Would you take care of my new friend Miles for a few minutes?"

Jimmy Rey, long black hair and wild, mismatched clothes, walked over in a slow, easy stride. "You play much volleyball?" he asked Miles. He turned away from the hand that Miles offered. Jimmy Rey rarely shook hands.

Mira could hear Miles' response fade as they walked away. "Usually it's softball for me," he was saying. "I just joined a league...."

Mira rushed to catch up with Jayson and Riley. Riley was telling a lawyer joke. He thought that was funny, to tell her lawyer jokes knowing she was studying for the bar exam. She thought he was doing it now to get a rise out of her. She must have made him mad.

"A terrorist, a lawyer and a rattlesnake are trapped in a plane with you. You have a gun with only two bullets. What do you do?"

"What?" Jayson filled in.

"Shoot the lawyer twice. Some things you can't be too sure of." Riley guffawed at his own telling of the joke. Mira glanced at

Jayson. He was successfully ignoring Riley.

The three of them climbed to the top of a tall hill that gave them a view of the craggy hills, fields dotted with wildflowers and the Firebrand River flowing through it. Beyond a dense stand of brush and trees at the back of her property, Mira could see development of what she had been told was some sort of resort. It looked like a large hotel, with six out-buildings. Around its perimeter, they were constructing on a wall. It wasn't the type of wall that encouraged community. It was tall and solid, made of metal and cement blocks.

"The owners of the resort had quite a time with platting and building permits. They kept insisting that the river was on their property," Riley said. "Your property manager, he took care of it. He was a pit bull about it. They wanted to put in a golf course that ran up to the river's edge, nine holes on their side and nine holes on your side, but Rossi was having none of it."

"Yeah, I remember signing a few legal documents." Mira thought that Riley was like her father, sociable and easy-going, but Riley worked hard. Dad had been always looking for the easy way. Mira believed that this fault in her father's character was behind her parents' divorce as much as anything else. One too many times, child-like behavior like Riley's turned into childish behavior like Dad's. It must have been frustrating for a wife to live with.

"You know that this land is not up for sale. I haven't thought about selling it." *Yet*, thought Mira. She hadn't told anybody about the job offer in Memphis. Whether it was Memphis or not, she would be unlikely to find her first real job in Austin. Chances were, she would have to move somewhere else soon.

Of course, she could keep the land where ever she lived. Mira didn't hang on to the land because she believed it would one day be worth a lot of money. She kept it because it was a gift from her father and she had too little else of him.

Jayson pointed to the top of a neighboring hill. "There's a man watching us using binoculars."

Mira searched until she saw the man. He turned away and lay down on the grass. "Yeah. We see him sometimes. Jimmy Rey had a talk with him."

Jayson raised an eyebrow and waited for her to go on.

"He says he's a birdwatcher. He likes the painted buntings, but he said he has also seen bald eagles a couple times."

"Huh." Jayson smiled at her in a way that lit up his eyes. He pulled a small spiral notebook from his shirt pocket and wrote a number on a piece of paper. He handed it to Mira.

She looked at it. It was a dollar amount almost twice the value of her land. "Why?" she asked.

Riley leaned over her shoulder, trying to steal a glance at the note. When that didn't work, he attempted to take the paper from her hand.

Mira gripped it and pulled it away from him. She put it into her pocket.

"Don't I get to see?" Riley asked.

"My company is speculating," Jayson said, ignoring Riley. "They have a good feeling about this area." He glanced at the resort with its confining wall and Mira wondered if Jayson's company was affiliated with the resort.

"Still, I don't think...."

"Just think about it. Will you promise me that?"

Mira thought it over for a few seconds. "I guess I can promise that."

Jayson walked away.

"Let me see," Riley whined.

"Grow up," Mira said.

"Come on." He tagged after her as she walked down the hill.

Chapter 7 - *Mira* - Saturday, April 25, 2026

Mira brought a bar review manual and a glass of iced tea with her. She sat in a webbed lawn chair by the water. After ten days of unpredictable weather: dark clouds, wind, both wet and dry thunderstorms and flooding, the current was quick in this part of the Firebrand River. It ran fast, getting caught on rocks and in crevices. She could see the current dragging tree limbs and other small debris to some unknown spot downstream. That was spring in Texas.

Jimmy Rey sat down next to her. He pulled his long black hair from his man-bun and shook it out. He was wearing purple calico shorts. Mira couldn't imagine where he purchased his clothes. Who made bright-colored calico shorts for men and tried to sell them? It must be another Jimmy Rey, someone whose taste in clothes is a little odd. Jimmy Rey didn't have on a shirt and his skin glistened from exertion, shimmering beads of sweat streamed down his bronze, hairless chest. Mira assumed he had just finished a volleyball game.

A hot afternoon breeze turned the leaves on the trees to show their silver undersides. On her property, there was mostly juniper, their branches extending like arthritic fingers, but here along the river, there were also many elms and oaks with Spanish moss hanging down. Mockingbirds, woodpeckers and grackles made these trees their home. She glanced over to see if any little black birds were out in the Purple Martin house and feeder that Jimmy Rey had erected last year. Instead, squirrels chased each other around the base while they searched for fallen seeds.

Upriver, there was a cove where the water became deep, about fifteen feet after the recent rain. Jimmy Rey had tied a rope to one of the trees and Mira watched as several boys swung out over the water and fell with a splash. The boys chattered and laughed. A dog, out for the day, barked at them.

"Did you bring your canoe out this weekend?" Mira asked.

Jimmy Rey took a gulp of water. He didn't answer her question, and instead went to the topic that was on his mind. "I heard you got an offer on this place. I didn't know it was for sale."

"I didn't have it on the market. This guy," she pointed to Jayson as he fought for the ball at the net, "called out of the blue." Mira waved her hand toward the construction across the river. "I'm guessing his company has something to do with that monstrosity."

"Are you going to sell?"

"If I decide to sell, you'll be the first to know."

Mira and Jimmy Rey didn't talk about it, but both considered this place part his. He had made it his own.

Mira had stayed in a small tent the first couple months, but as the party expanded, it became clear that wouldn't work on a long-term basis. Jimmy Rey was a carpenter by trade. He and some of the other volleyball players built a little cabin for her: living room, bedroom, kitchen and bath. He built it under the trees not far from to the river, but out of the flood zone. It was quiet, removed from the volleyball court. She could retreat and be in peace while the games went on. The front of the house faced east, so the early morning sunrise greeted her at daybreak as she opened the shutters on the window or the door.

By unwritten rule, no one except Jimmy Rey stayed in the cabin when she was not there. She thought these stays were becoming more and more frequent.

Jimmy Rey had made other improvements as well. He laid a gravel drive from the highway on the west side of the property ending in parking for a dozen cars. A cable fence prevented people from parking haphazardly all over her land, crushing the grass and disturbing the wildlife.

Later, Jimmy Rey and his friends built a second cabin that

housed a sink, a refrigerator and a full three-piece bathroom. Mysteriously, a jar appeared in this second cabin and, as people came inside to catch a shower, they threw a dollar or two into the jar for the water and electricity. They had talked about solar panels, but the initial cost was still beyond their means. Jimmy Rey kept track of the money in the jar. After paying for the utilities, if anything was left over, he went to Dottie's to buy bottled water and beer for the refrigerator.

"This grassy area is getting high. I'll mow it next week," Jimmy Rey said.

Mira looked out over the tall grass. Bluebonnets, poppies and Indian paintbrush dotted the field with color. "Wait a couple of weeks, until the flowers die out."

He nodded in confirmation. Slow-moving fiery air lifted the coal-black hair from Jimmy Rey's forehead. He gathered it up and secured it with a covered band.

Mira loved Jimmy Rey like family. He had the serenity of a man that had nothing to prove. He was genuinely kind and helpful. Whenever he saw something that needed to be done, he just did it. Mira thought he loved her as a friend as well. She hoped it wasn't more for him. She would do anything in the world not to hurt him.

"I don't want to sell," Mira said. She had been thinking about leaving the land in Jimmy Rey's hands if she decided to move.

Jimmy Rey nodded, finished off his bottle of water, and then returned to the volleyball game.

Andee took his seat. She turned her lawn chair to be able to better watch the game.

Mira looked at her and finished the thought she had started with Jimmy Rey, "I don't much care about playing volleyball anymore."

Andee looked at her like she was nuts. "Then don't."

Mira turned her chair forty-five degrees so she could see the volleyball as well. Miles was playing. He had a competitive soul, but obviously wasn't practiced at the game. He had taken off his shirt displaying a long, sinewy, pale torso. Even though he had been trying to stay in the shade when possible, his skin had taken on a rosy glow.

"Who's the handsome one?" Andee asked.

"Miles?"

"Blue eyes, blond hair. Corporate. I'd go after him if I was you."

"Oh. Jayson Brookshire. He's cute, but he's not the handsome one."

Andee laughed. "Oh yeah."

"Jayson Brookshire's employer wants to buy this place."

Andee looked alarmed.

"I haven't decided to sell," Mira quickly added.

"Then why's he still here?"

"Why else? He wanted to play volleyball."

"I don't know about that. He's paying more attention to you than the game.

"You're imagining things." Mira glanced at Jayson. He was distracting, but she found her eyes being drawn back to Miles.

Mira followed Andee's gaze to the lagoon. She stared at the river toward the pool where the small children liked to watch the guppies. It looked odd. "Does something look off to you?" She tilted her head. She wasn't sure. They walked over for a closer look.

Six-year old Maddox Roget was laughing and shouting as he splashed in the water. He excitedly yelled to her, "The water is green."

Mira sucked in her breath. The air smelled foul, like decay. She saw a dead fish floating, trapped in putrid water that was, as Maddox said, a brilliant shade of green.

Five-year-old Hollis Jones jumped in the water and held out his hands like a monster covered in oil.

"Out of the water," Juliette Roget, Maddox's mom, yelled at

the boys. "I told you that you couldn't swim this weekend. Get out."

They ignored her as they stood in the shallows.

"Get out of the water, Maddox," she repeated.

Juliette marched the two little boys, dragging them by the elbows, up the hill, and into the second cabin. The boys screamed and shouted at her, drawing the attention of the volleyball players.

Mira turned on the shower, stepped in and she and Juliette lathered them in soap with clothes and then without.

"Do you have a change of clothes for Maddox?" Mira asked.

"I think so."

Miles opened the cabin door and stood in the entryway.

"Will you get them, please?" Mira asked. "And see if Hollis' mom has some extras too."

Juliette nodded and moved past Miles as he entered the cabin.

"The lagoon looks rancid," Mira said. "Will you get some of the parents to help. Run to the cove downstream where the older boys play on the rope swing and get them out of the water and into a shower."

Through the door, Mira could already see Juliette running toward her older son, Nathan, and yelling something Mira could not hear clearly.

Miles took off at speed toward Juliette.

When Maddox and Hollis were clean and redressed, Mira joined the crowd gathering at the firepit. She urgently recommended to the parents whose kids had been swimming that they take their children home and give them a long, hot bath with lots of soap. The parents did.

Chapter 8 - *Riley* - Saturday, April 25, 2026

The sun was setting as many of the volleyball players packed up to leave. Riley watched Mira in animated conversation with Jimmy Rey. That guy Miles was still here too. The three of them walked Mira's property line, ending in a grassy field full of wildflowers. Jimmy Rey and Miles ambled off toward the river. Mira stood at the far edge of the field making phone calls. The fading sun picked up the red highlights in her auburn hair. Normally, she walked fluidly with a slight sway, but, this evening, she looked tense, her muscles tight and unresponsive.

Riley walked toward her picking a small bundle of wild flowers along the way. When he reached her, he held them out like a shy little boy. He had to resist the urge to hang his head and kick a clod of dirt with his shoe.

Mira took them. A good start. "I love flowers," she said. "Thank you."

"Oh shucks," he said. He looked in her deep brown eyes and wouldn't yield her gaze. She looked worried and unhappy. "Is everything okay?"

"Would you be in on the sale," Mira asked, "since Alonzo Rossi couldn't make it today?"

"No. Bringing Brookshire out. That was just a favor. I would rather you didn't sell," he said. "You know, Mira. I'm not joking about us as a couple. Any chance you might be serious too?"

Mira's face flushed, giving him more answer than he wanted.

He rushed on. "I love you and I want you to marry me. Will you?" He knew the answer, so he started his arguments before she had a chance to respond. "I have a good job. I can provide security, protection. I can support you while you start your law practice. I want children and I'll make a good father. We could be a family. I want a family." Riley took Mira's hand and fell to one knee. "Say yes. Say yes, please, please, please."

Mira persuaded him up off his knees. "Riley, I'm really flattered. I think you're special, but…."

"Just don't say no." He rushed away at a pace just short of racing. "Don't say no."

"Riley, come back," she called after him. "We need to talk about this."

He reached the parking lot and climbed into his car.

"I'm late for work," he called back to her.

Riley arrived at work about two hours later, but only thirty minutes late. He was to sit in a model home from six o'clock to nine o'clock that evening. He hadn't been scheduled until Monday, but that mysteriously changed yesterday. He suspected Alonzo Rossi of tampering with his schedule to keep him away from Mira and his land deal.

Riley turned on his phone and checked for messages. No one was looking for him. The real estate market had been shallow lately and he hadn't sold a home in too long.

Rossi showed up about eight o'clock. He looked ragged with dark circles under his eyes and a pale pallor. He had a cigarette in his hand. Riley didn't think that Rossi smoked. That was new.

"How ya feeling, Al?" Riley asked. Alonzo gave him a look. He didn't like being called 'Al" and he likely knew it was a dig.

Alonzo lit a new cigarette from the old one. "I feel like shit. Had the runs for eight hours straight. Thanks for taking that guy out to see that piece of property."

"No problem. You want a soda? Might help settle your stomach."

Alonzo didn't answer, but Riley decided that was a "yes."

Riley shook his head as he got a Diet Coke for himself and a Sprite for Al from a mini-frig.

He probably put too much laxative into Al's coffee that morning. Alonzo looked really out of it. Riley only wanted him to feel sick for a couple of hours, payback for changing the schedule and long enough for him to get Jayson Brookshire away from Mira.

"How'd it go with Brookshire? Did he make an offer?"

"Not sure," Riley said. "He said something to Mira, but she didn't give him an answer. Worried about the loss of a big commission?" he snickered.

Alonzo ignored him.

"Why don't you go lay down for a few minutes? I'll call you if anyone comes in," Riley offered.

Alonzo took a giant sip of his soda and then dragged himself, feet shuffling, into the master bedroom of the model home. "Thanks, man."

Riley gave him a few minutes to settle in and fall asleep. When he heard Al's nasal breathing and throaty snore, he opened Al's briefcase and searched its contents. Riley casually read through a few files about Mira's property. Jayson worked for a development company called Andover and Associates. Andover seemed to be associated with the Wagner Company in a way that Riley couldn't quite figure out.

The head of the both companies had recently died. Riley had heard about it on the news. There was a new flu virus that just appeared in New Jersey where the men were meeting. Maybe the deaths had something to do with the rush to buy.

Alonzo's car keys were in the case. Riley peeked in the bedroom to ensure that his co-worker was sound asleep before he took the keys. He went outside and searched the trunk of Alonzo's car.

Chapter 9 - *Mira* - Saturday, April 25, 2026

"So how did this whole weekend party thing get started?" Miles asked Mira. They walked along the river watching the quality of the water as it flowed and tumbled past the flower-covered hill on the far bank. The sun was setting behind the hill.

Mira remembered the first weekend she came out to the land. It was almost a year after her father died. She planned to camp for the weekend. She wanted Andee to come with her, but Andee was fighting it every step of the way.

Mira packed a tarp, two sleeping bags, and a frying pan. In a plastic bin, she added toilet paper, hot dogs and the ingredients for smores. Finally, Andee had relented and agreed to come with her. Andee would do anything for chocolate.

They tied the tarp between three trees near the river's edge, and angled it to protect them from the afternoon sun. Mira raked the ground with her shoe to clear the rocks and other debris from under the cover. They sat on their sleeping bags.

"What's that?" Andee insisted she heard something.

"You're paranoid. You know that?"

They took a swim in the river and Andee thought she saw something moving in the trees.

Mira teased. "It's probably a bear," but then Mira saw it too, a large shadowy figure hidden in the trees. "You've got to stop this. You're making me paranoid too. It's just a deer."

Near dark, they made a rock circle and built a fire. They found sharp sticks to cook their hot dogs. The temperature dropped ten degrees in ten minutes. The wind picked up. The clouds burst and sheets of rain fell. It looked like gray silk flowing down.

They moved what they could to the car to keep it dry, but they and all their stuff smelled moldy and stale.

"My point exactly," Andee said.

An old tan pickup with a camper shell drove out of the woods and parked tail-first at the end of their tarp. A long-haired man in a rain poncho got out, opened the rear camper door. He smiled. He fixed their rain-soaked tarp by adding canopy poles and restarted their fire. Next to the fire he lit a lantern and hung it from one canopy's pole. He sat on the truck's tailgate and motioned for them to come over and join him.

They hesitated.

"Bring any dry food?" he asked.

Mira grabbed her bin and joined him. As the rain slacked off, Andee followed.

Jimmy Rey took off his rain wear. He had on a red fishnet tank top and rose-pink shorts that hurt the eyes. Andee laughed and covered her mouth with her hand.

They sat on a pad in the back of his truck, talked, told stories. They ate graham crackers and chocolate bars and eventually huddled together and fell asleep.

In the morning, the bright sun was well on the way to drying out their things. Mira made eggs in her cast iron pan over the fire, and then Jimmy Rey took them on a canoe ride up the river.

Mira smiled remembering that day, and so Miles did too. "Spontaneously," Mira answered Miles question.

Chapter 10 - *Mira* - Saturday, April 25, 2026

It was full dark now. Jimmy Rey had gone out foraging for dry wood. With the fire pit going full blast most weekend nights, he had to go further and further into the underbrush to find fuel. The side effect was that he was systematically clearing the undergrowth from her land. He was near finished, except for the furthest fifteen acres which he had never touched.

Miles pulled a dead branch toward the fire pit. Jimmy Rey's chain saw wasn't working, so they started at opposite ends using hand saws to reduce the branch into bonfire-sized logs. When they were done, Jimmy Rey built the fire.

"How about roasting hot dogs," Mira said. "I'll make a salad." She headed for the cabin.

Sometimes, they liked to go all out on the food–make a gourmet meal–but this wasn't one of those days. She'd freeze the chicken and save it for next weekend.

While she created a dressing and tossed it into the salad, Jimmy Rey came into the kitchen. He munched on a carrot.

"What did Riley want?" he asked.

"He wants me to marry him and have his babies."

"What else is new?"

Jimmy Rey was worried about the idea of her selling the land. Mira could see it in his eyes.

Mira asked Jimmy Rey the thing she'd often wondered. "Where do you live?"

He said nothing. Quiet was an art form for Jimmy Rey. Mira knew it was best with men like that not to question him straight out, but to dance around the subject until he was ready to bring it up, but Jimmy Rey never had—likely never would.

"I think you might live here on this land," Mira said. "I think you stay in the cabin when I'm gone. I don't think you have another address."

He looked down. "I'll move."

"You must know I don't care." She touched his hand. "After all, you were here first." Mira could see it behind his eyes. She hadn't used a label like homeless or trespasser, but she felt sure he would need to do something to correct the situation. "Please stay," she said. "I love having a caretaker here when I'm in town."

"Okay," he said and the look lightened a little, "but I want to pay rent."

"I should be paying you for all the work you do around here. I need you. Can we call it a trade, like we've been doing?"

Jimmy Rey beamed showing all his white teeth.

Mira gave him a hug.

They carried the food outside to a picnic table near the fire pit, but they each took a camping chair near the fire. Mira jammed her dog on a stick and began roasting it.

"What do you think I should do about the river?" she asked.

Jimmy Rey watched her in that thoughtful way he had as her dog began to spit, but it was Miles who supplied an answer.

"Get a lab to test the water, see what you're dealing with. I'd call the police and see what they can arrange for you. I can help with that.

Mira nodded. "Can't call anyone until Monday. I tried."

Miles took up his water bottle and poured the contents on his hands. He winced and looked at his fingers, so Mira did too. They were dirty, dry, cracked, and bleeding in one place from the work of sawing the logs. It hurt her just to look at them.

"Come into the house," she said. "Let me put some antiseptic on that cut." She handed her cooked hot dog to Andee and walked toward the cabin. He followed her.

At the kitchen sink, he scrubbed his hands and face. Mira sprayed antiseptic on the cut and put a Ninja Turtles bandage on it. His hands were remarkably dry. She got a bottle of lotion from her bathroom and poured some into her hand. She took his hand and massaged the lotion into his parched skin, avoiding the cut. He allowed it. His look of tolerance gave way to a soft smile.

"Thanks," he said.

"Want me to do the other one?"

"Yeah."

Again, she squirted the lotion into her palm and took his hand. She rolled her fingertips around each of his fingers releasing the musky fragrance of the cream.

We've been moving toward sex since the first second that we laid eyes on each other, she thought. She took her slick hands and gently smoothed them across his sunburnt forehead and nose.

"That's really slimy," he commented.

But not yet, she thought. She took the bottle of lotion into the bathroom and put it away.

As she turned from the cabinet, she slammed right into Miles. Knocked off balance, she placed her hand on his shoulder. They were standing very close and she was touching him. Mira struggled to get words out of her mouth, not the least of which might be "excuse me" or "I'm sorry," but no words escaped her lips.

He pulled back, looking uncertain.

She had to rein herself in. She was thinking soulmates

and all he may see was a highly receptive female who picked him up at breakfast.

She nodded toward the door. "Let's take a walk," she said.

She went out the door and up the hill. Miles followed her in silence. The quiet was nice. She was enjoying the peace and the time alone with him.

After a dozen minutes of quiet walking, Miles stopped. "There's something you ought to know," he said.

Miles never completed his thought. Shrieking cut the night.

Chapter 11 - *Andee* – Saturday, April 25, 2026

Andee saw Mira and Miles walk away from the cabin. Jimmy Rey leveled a gaze at her and then he went inside. She glanced around. A guilty look on her face, but she followed him in.

Jimmy Rey sat on the bed. He looked at her from intense dark eyes. He smiled, only one side of his mouth turning up. He hadn't lowered the lighting or pulled back the bedclothes the way he might have done in the middle of the week. On weekdays, this was his home. Tonight's was to be a stolen moment that left things in Mira's house untouched.

Andee went to him. She forced him to lay back, his arms on the flannel-cased pillows over his head. He sprawled on the blue and white quilt that Mira's grandmother had made. Andee sat on his stomach and held down his arms.

"Cry for mercy," she said.

"No."

She sucked his mouth into hers and forced his lips to part.

He yelled out in pain, jumped from the bed and knocked her to the floor.

Andee struggled to her feet and watched him flail his arms in a strange dance, something long and dark hung down like a misplaced tail.

"What is it?" she pleaded.

"A snake," he yelled.

She could see it now. A snake was clamped down on

his forearm.

She opened the door and shrieked into the night. "Help. Somebody please," her voice went high-pitched. Andee struggled to master her panic and fear.

Jimmy Rey ran into the kitchen and grabbed a cleaver. He handed the cleaver to her. He laid his arm on the kitchen counter and pulled long the tail of the snake.

"Hold still," she commanded ignoring her own panic. She looked into his eyes until he signaled that he was ready. She brought the cleaver down hard, cutting off the top half of the serpent. Jimmy Rey pulled the head from his arm.

Mira and Miles pushed through the cabin door taking in the scene — Jimmy Rey's obvious pain and Andee's fear.

"Damn," Miles said looking at the decapitated snake. "Cottonmouth. That's not good. Stay completely still, okay?"

Miles forced Jimmy Rey onto the bed and held his arm motionless until he calmed and quit struggling against him.

Mira called 911. "I need a helicopter pickup to the hospital. We're about eighty miles outside of Austin and we have a snakebite. A cottonmouth."

Andee turned away seeking to gain control of her face. She wanted to look and sound calm for Jimmy Rey, but she felt far from it.

Miles explained as he took charge. "It's likely that whatever is polluting the Firebrand River made whatever could come out of the water do so, hence the snake."

Andee was thankful for Miles who seemed to know what he was doing. She removed Jimmy Rey's watch while Miles tied his own belt into a tight tourniquet around Jimmy Rey's arm.

"Get me a washcloth with some ice in it," Miles ordered Mira. "There's a first aid kit in my car." He tossed his keys to Andee and she rushed to get it.

Each step seemed to take an hour even though Andee was running. The inside of Miles' car was clean and mostly empty, except for an umbrella and a box of Kleenex. She tried the trunk. It was full of junk. Besides the spare tire and jack, there was an ice scraper, a small toolbox, and a bat, ball and glove. She pulled things from the trunk and threw them on the ground. His laundry, which had been clean and folded into a basket, ended up all over the yard. In the back of the trunk, she spotted the first aid kit. She ran back to the cabin.

Miles looked in the kit, but didn't find what he wanted. He took the antiseptic Mira had used earlier on the cut on his hand and sprayed Jimmy Rey's whole arm. He put the washcloth containing the ice close to the wound, but not actually on it.

Andee knelt beside the bed and took Jimmy Rey's hand. "You're okay, Hun. Help's on the way." Jimmy Rey looked pale and he was sweating. Andee brushed the hair from his forehead. She smiled reassuringly. She leaned in to him and kissed Jimmy Rey's forehead. *Please let him be okay,* she thought over and over.

"Snakes often hold back on the venom flow when they bite. They save some for later." Miles spoke calmly. He put a pillow under Jimmy Rey's arm and put a blanket over him. "That's why snake bites are so seldom fatal." He looked at Jimmy Rey. "You're not going to die."

What if the snake wasn't holding back, Andee wondered. "He's in pain." She could hear the hysteria in her own voice. She knew that from the look on Jimmy Rey's face.

Miles said nothing.

The helicopter finally arrived. Emergency technicians

jumped out and began to appraise the situation. "Good thing for him you knew what to do? He got any relatives here?"

"No. Take her." Miles pushed Andee forward.

Mira stared at Miles, her jaw dropped. "I wanted to go with him. Jimmy Rey is my special friend."

Andee hesitated.

"He's like a brother to me." Mira stood in stunned silence.

"Did you see Andee's face? They're a couple."

Miles helped Andee climb into the helicopter.

Chapter 12 – *Mira* - Sunday – April 26, 2026

They had been waiting for hours in a glass cubicle the hospital called the visitor's center. It was packed with family members—standing room only. Most reported that their loved-ones seemed to have flu-like symptoms. Mira sucked in her breath, reminded of the worst of COVID.

At first, there had been nurses with forms and a doctor who made non-committal statements about Jimmy Rey's health, but soon there was just the waiting. "Wait and see." That's what the doctor had said. "Come back in the morning." That's what the nurses wanted, but neither she nor Andee had the will to leave.

It was still dark out the window when Mira awoke feeling guilty because she had fallen asleep and left Andee alone. Mira could see Andee sitting on a formed plastic chair in a corner looking stiff and beaten, but wide awake.

There was a disturbance in the hallway. A nurse had a patient on a gurney. The patient looked at death's door – pale, sweaty, gasping for his every breath.

A young nurse came to help.

The first nurse held out her gloved hand. Stop. "Put on your mask and face shield," she instructed.

The second nurse looked hesitant.

"Put on your mask or go home." The first nurse got tough, and so the second nurse put on her gear.

Mira stood. She joined the tough nurse. "What's going on."

"A doctor from Mexico came in with a flu-bug. Nothing to worry about. People get the flu every year."

Mira didn't believe her.

After the nurse left, she looked at the shut door, afraid

of what was behind it.

Mira found a used newspaper on one of the chairs in the waiting room. She read about a flu that seemed to have started almost simultaneously on the eastern coast and in Mexico. It was spreading in clusters across North America. The flu was fast-moving, probably air borne, with a short incubation period – maybe three or four days. People were getting sick. Again.

Mira went to the nurses' station and asked for a few N95 masks which they seemed happy to provide. They gave her gloves as well. She walked back to the waiting area.

She jostled Andee to get her attention. "We should go."

"No. No. I'm staying. You go."

Mira sighed and sat back down.

There was a bottle of hand sanitizer on an end table. Mira squirted her hands with the sanitizer and put on her mask, but Andee simply held hers in one hand. Mira took the mask from Andee's hand, rubbed some sanitizer on her hands, and then put the mask over her mouth and nose. Andee didn't protest.

Miles returned in the pre-dawn hours of the morning. Mira handed him a N95 face mask and he put it on.

Mira stretched out on a vinyl sofa with her head resting on Miles' thigh. He rubbed her back.

"Mira, are you awake?" Miles asked. The sun lit the room. She must have fallen back to sleep.

She sat up. "Yes. Has anything happened?"

"No." He knew what she meant. "I have to go to work."

"Okay."

"Do you want me to take you home. You need some

sleep."

"No, thank you."

"But neither one of you drove here. You have no car."

"My car is still at the restaurant. I'll take an Uber to it."

"Are you sure?"

Mira nodded again and wished he wouldn't go. She touched her hand to his chest.

"Mira."

"Yes?"

"May I have your phone number?"

She laughed at the absurdity of the question, and then felt guilty for laughing. She fumbled with his phone and entered her number. He took it from her and then texted his number back. He stood, smiled down at her and was gone.

Mira looked again at Andee. She faded into the corner, looking insignificant. Mira held out her hand.

"Will you come sit with me?"

Andee did as she was told. Mira wrapped her arms around Andee's shoulders and pulled her in. Andee resisted for a second, and then rested her head on Mira's shoulder. Small sobs racked her body. Mira murmured reassurances and stroked her hair. After a while, Andee stilled, but they clung to the comfort of each other's arms.

"Why didn't you tell me about you and Jimmy Rey?" Mira asked.

"At first, Jimmy Rey didn't want me to. I was going to tell you at breakfast yesterday. Before you picked up some random guy."

"Aren't you glad now that I did." Mira sat silently for a minute. "But why," she asked, "wouldn't Jimmy Rey want me to know about you two?"

"I don't know for sure, but I guess he thought it would change things between us and you. He didn't want that."

Mira couldn't help but notice that Andee put her and Jimmy Rey in one group and Mira separate.

"You know I love Jimmy Rey, but we're only friends."

"Yes, I know."

Mira waited hoping she would say more.

"Every Wednesday night, I go with him," Andee said reluctantly, "to a place."

"What place?"

"Hello my name is Jimmy Rey."

"A.A.? I know Jimmy Rey has had some trouble in the past. Why do you go?"

"I was tired of feeling alone. I told Jimmy Rey one Saturday. I told him about my father." Andee's dad was a drinker. And then later, her brother was too. She rarely talked about either of them.

"He invited me to come with him. He's been going for six years. I've been going to the other support group for a couple months. It's good."

"I didn't know that."

"There's a lot you don't know about Jimmy Rey, but you'll have to ask him about that."

Mira kissed the top of her friend's head and pondered all the things she didn't know.

Chapter 13 – *Jayson* - Sunday, April 26, 2026

Jayson wasn't sleeping well. He woke in the middle of the night with his heart racing. *Am I having a heart attack?* he worried. He rubbed his jaw with shaking hands, sore from clenching his teeth. He couldn't afford to crack another molar.

He was troubled about this land deal. His boss had been on his case like at no other time. The man's tension was palpable, and so then was his. Jayson felt that there must be a lot at stake. If he pulled off this deal, maybe he'd be up for a big bonus or a promotion. If not, maybe he couldn't afford to live in this nice new condo with its giant window and view of Lady Bird Lake.

Mira was an obstacle, a revelation and a surprise. She was smart and cautious. She surrounded herself with people who cared about her, watched over her, and he could see why. She was the heart of their group. He had watched her all afternoon and concluded that she found castaways and gave them a place in the world — her world, a kind, loving place. He couldn't help but want to be a part of that world too, even as he wanted to rob her of it.

Well before the morning light began its streak across his bedroom window, he got up. He put on shorts, a tank top and his trainers and went into the kitchen. He filled the well on the coffee maker with bottled water and set the timer for forty-five minutes, allowing himself time for a quick run around the lake.

The path came almost up to his building's front door. The trail was wide, fairly easy, and sheltered by a dome of trees. Birds sang and water lapped the shore. The only real obstacle was the other pre-dawn runners, bikers and walkers. He dodged them left and right.

By the end of his run, he'd doubled-up on his mileage, but the coffee machine had kept his brew warm. He took a sip. He turned on the news as he wondered if Mira would still be at the river. He thought about what she would like, what might get her attention, and so he dressed just like Miles had the day before. Mira clearly liked him.

Something on television about snakes caught his attention.

"Huh?" he said.

He grabbed his car keys.

Chapter 14 – *Mira* - Sunday, April 26, 2026

The sun grayed the dark outside the Jimmy Rey's hospital window. A nurse wearing scrubs, gloves and a N95 mask fluttered around the second bed in the room. She changed sheets, getting it ready for a new occupant.

"This morning, his color is good," Andee told the nurse, smiling at Jimmy Rey through eyes that still held her concern of the night before.

Mira stood in a far corner.

"Doctor says you can go home this morning, "the nurse told Jimmy Rey. "You'll be out of here within the hour or so. You're too healthy now to take up a bed in this hospital with this new flu going around."

"So early?" Mira asked. "Has the doctor even been in?"

"Believe me, he'll be better out of here, at home in his own bed," the nurse said.

Jimmy Rey had a lot of friends, many of which Mira didn't know. About eight o'clock in the morning, they began to arrive at the glass cube to sit on the plastic furniture waiting in turn to look in on him. *Visiting hours,* she thought.

Mira stood in the corner of the waiting room while other friends looked in on Jimmy Rey, her butt too sore to sit on the hard furniture another minute.

The television was on in the corner. Rory Burke, the red-headed newscaster on KNUS, was talking about the virus identified in New Jersey, and how transmissible it was. Rory was reviewing lessons learned from COVID-19 about wearing masks, washing hands and staying out of crowds.

Mira looked around the crowded room and pushed

down her fear.

Mira slipped out of he waiting room. She went to the cafeteria and bought a coffee. Now that she was more certain that Jimmy Rey would be fine, her mind switched to other concerns, the water quality on her land being one of them. She wanted to get to the bottom of the sludge in the lagoon.

Mira sat at a table and pulled a pad of paper from her backpack. She did a data search on her phone for 'cottonmouth' and found an article about how snakes will crawl ashore if the water environment is compromised.

She flipped through her phone's data on 'water quality' and made a list of possible options for help: County Water Control and Improvement, the Municipal Utility District, State Department of Health, State Parks and Recreation, and State Natural Resources Conservation Commission. She wrote an email to the Texas Commission on Environment Quality briefly describing the situation and attaching a picture from her phone of the river's state.

Andee joined her in the cafeteria, popping the top on a soda. "There's not enough caffeine in the world this morning. I'm exhausted."

Mira said, "I've made a list of agencies who might be able to tell us more about the river. As soon as they're open, I'll start calling."

"If you're worried about it…" She stopped talking. Mira was surprised when Jayson Brookshire joined them.

"It's in the news." Jayson answered Mira's silent question about how he knew to come to the hospital. "A cottonmouth on the Firebrand River. How's he doing?" Jayson asked.

"Much better this morning. We got him to the hospital in time."

Jayson nodded his approval.

"Jimmy Rey's sensitivity to venom was mild," Mira told Jayson, "and the drugs they gave him pulled him through."

Jayson felt ill at ease as he offered his support in platitudes. "I'm sure he'll be fine. Ready for the next volleyball game."

"I stopped by his room. Jimmy Rey says he can leave at any time, I was wondering if you need a lift."

"That would be nice, if it's not too much trouble." Andee said.

The three of them and a nurse escorted Jimmy Rey in his wheelchair outside. Mira and Andee waited by the front curb while Jayson went to get his car. The drive was mostly silent.

Jayson dropped the three of them at Mira's car. He had a nice new Jeep and Mira enjoyed the luxury of riding in it. She wanted to play with the gizmos and gadgets, but she thought that would be disrespectful.

Jayson got out of his car with the rest of them and helped Jimmy Rey get settled into the back of Mira's old Chevy Volt. When they were ready to go, Jayson stood near Mira and hemmed his words.

"You got a nasty note." He pointed to a few angry words scrawled on paper and left on her front window.

Mira looked toward the spot where the angry woman stood watching on her front porch. "I guess that's not surprising."

"You haven't said anything yet about my offer for your land. Would you like to have dinner later and discuss it?"

"Let's see how the day goes," she said slowly, apprehensively. Mira wondered if he was asking her to dinner as an excuse to discuss the sale of the land or suggesting discussion of the land as an excuse to take her to dinner.

Jayson waved as he got into his car. He put on his seatbelt and drove away.

"I don't think I trust that guy," Andee said.

"Something's not right," Jimmy Rey echoed.

"Why? What do you mean? He seems like a nice enough man to me," though she was apprehensive too.

Mira took Jimmy Rey and Andee to Andee's apartment where she could pamper him. Andee lived in a grouping of four-plexes. Visible between the buildings were a small park with a playscape and a swimming pool.

Mira hadn't been to Andee's in some time. There were subtle differences. Large, heavy work boots sat by the potted begonias near the front door.

Without asking, Jimmy Rey happily climbed into Andee's rumpled bed and lay back on the pillows. Andee was a stickler about making her bed.

"Can I get you anything," Mira asked.

"Maybe a glass of water," Jimmy Rey said.

The glasses, cups, and spoons in the sink waiting to be washed were multiplied by two. Needle nose pliers, a Phillips head screwdriver and some washers sat on the kitchen counter by the faucet. Mira held up the screwdriver and looked at Andee.

"He offered to fix a leak," Andee said as she followed Mira into the kitchen.

"Uh huh. That's not all the plumbing he's taking care of around here."

Mira felt uncomfortable, like an interloper. She suspected she was unwanted and didn't like the feeling. Maybe Jimmy Rey was right. Mira didn't want things to change. She wanted everything to remain as it was. Still, she kissed Andee on the cheek and headed out.

Chapter 15 – *Mira* - Sunday, April 26, 2026

Mira's little apartment seemed almost foreign to her, like a crowded closet lived in by a stranger with a whole different life. She couldn't shake her lack of ease. Her life felt off. She felt off. She pushed all the clothes from her bed, took a hot shower, and then fell naked and damp on top of her sheets and covers into a deep sleep.

She thought she was dreaming the sound of her own running feet, and then her hands beating against a barred door, but soon she realized that someone was actually knocking at her door. She looked at her clock. It wasn't yet noon. She had barely gotten two hours of sleep since she got home from the hospital.

"Just a minute," she croaked, her voice not fully awake yet either. She stretched, yawned and then got up. She put on the nearest clothes – a pair of dirty jeans and a wrinkled tee shirt.

She peeked out and then opened the door, leaving the screen door locked.

"Flowers, Ma'am." The delivery guy held out a bouquet of a dozen pure white roses.

She unlatched the screen door and took them, making a space for them on the desk.

"Let me get you a tip," she said.

"That's not necessary," the deliveryman said.

Mira watched him go and then found a card. She read, "I hope you will take my offer to heart and say you will marry me. Riley."

Mira was growing suspicious of all this sudden attention. She hadn't dated much at all in the last year. Now she had three men in hot pursuit.

Mira lay on her bed and stared at the ceiling. She picked up a textbook, but couldn't concentrate. She didn't delude herself that she could go back to sleep, so she got up. She threw on some clean clothes, grabbed her car keys and drove out to the land down by the river.

When Mira arrived, trash was strewn all over the ground. She was mad until she remembered that Andee had searched Miles car looking for the first aid kit. These must be the items from the trunk that were likely flung all over the place by the helicopter. Mira picked up a white shirt that was no longer clean. It was damp from an early morning rain. She put it with other clothes she gathered into a laundry basket she assumed was Miles'. She added the softball, bat and glove. She'd have to remember to return them.

Mira walked to the water's edge and up-righted a lawn chair left there the day before. She sat down. Except for the wind in the leaves and the chattering of squirrels, it was quiet. The clouds looked like white airbrush against a blue canvas.

In the past, this had always been her place of peace and calm. It was a good place to think. Now, she felt ill at ease and stressed. She sat there for a long time trying to shake her growing sense of distrust.

She got up purposefully and walked around the cabin. When she felt safe enough, Mira went inside. She searched for snakes, but found none. She went through the recycling bin and pulled out several old glass jars with lids. She scrubbed them and dried them well before she put them into a basket.

The lagoon smelled as foul as it had the day before. It had a green glow rimmed by a nasty-looking foam. She filled a couple jars with the cove water, making certain to get both the green and the foam, and then filled another jar with the surrounding topsoil.

Mira looked up and saw the birdwatcher-man staring at her through binoculars. He wore heavy boots, jeans and a long-sleeved shirt even though it was hot. He removed his cap and mopped his rosy forehead with his arm. From this distance, Mira still couldn't see him clearly. He nodded and disappeared to the other side of the hill.

Mira stopped at Dottie's on her way back to town. Dottie was pushing a broom, clearing dust and tracked-in dirt from her front porch. Mira stood in the screen door and watched her. She looked old, showing every one of her years.

"Hey Chickee," Mira said.

"Hey yourself."

Mira grabbed a soda from the refrigerator and put it on the counter.

Dottie looked back in her mind. "Keep seein' a handsome young man on your property on weekdays. Who's that?"

"Not Jimmy Rey?"

"Naw. Seen him a time or two before. Know him?"

"Dottie, can you tell me in detail what this man looked like?"

"Didn't see much. I was just passing by, but like I said, I seen him before. He was young. That's easy enough to tell at my age. His movement was strong and easy. And he was handsome. That's why I looked."

"Can you be more specific?"

"Slim, had light-colored hair. That's really all I saw."

Mira thought about the men she knew who fit the description, including Jayson, Riley and Miles." She was in pain. She liked all three men and didn't want to suspect any of them of rotten deeds, but the pain was all about Miles. It can't be him. "Did you see the man who drove here with me yesterday? Stayed in the car."

"Sorry honey. I didn't see him."

Mira shook her head in disappointment. "I better hurry, get on the road," she said.

"Got a hot date?

"No telling how hot."

Chapter 16 – *Mira* - Sunday, April 26, 2026

Jayson picked up Mira about seven o'clock that evening. He arrived at the door of her dinky apartment wearing a black designer suit with a pale gray linen dress shirt and a black silk tie. He carried a spray of exotic flowers and a bottle of Merlot. Mira had on a nice blouse and jeans. They didn't look like they were going out together.

"Come in," Mira said, recognizing that she should have picked up her mess more.

Jayson handed her the flowers and wine as he passed her at the door.

"Thank you. I'll put these in water," she said. "Would you like to open the wine?"

The roses from Riley were on the desk–the only large flat surface in the room. She wondered where she would put a second arrangement. For now, she put Riley's flowers in the kitchen sink and put Jayson's flowers on the desk.

"If you'd like some too." He answered her question about the wine while taking in her whole apartment at a glance.

"I seem to be running a few minutes behind," she lied. "If you pour the wine, I'll pour myself into my dress."

"I came directly from work," he offered his own lie to make her feel better. He took off his tie and loosened his collar.

"You wear a suit when you work on Sunday?"

"I always wear a suit to the office."

"You look terrific." Very terrific, she thought. His blond hair looked almost white against the dark suit and the gray shirt brought out the pale blueness of his eyes. She rooted around in a drawer and pulled out a corkscrew. She placed it in his palm. "Just give me five minutes."

She stepped into her walk-in closet, shut the door and prayed that she could find something clean and appropriate. In the back, she found a purple cocktail-length dress she had worn to an evening wedding about a year before. Fine. It will do, she thought. She stripped down and pulled the dress over her head. She slipped on a pair of heels and marched into the room with Jayson, flashed him a smile and beat it into the bathroom. She darkened her lip color and eye shadow. That's the best you get, she thought. She opened the bathroom door and came out.

Jayson sat in her overstuffed chair, thumbing through the papers on her desk. Mira wondered if he had hit the space bar on her computer and looked in her history. If he had, he would see that she had done some unremarkable searches on the three men in her life and Andover and Associates, Jayson's employer. It seemed like a fairly large business with a sound financial picture, reputable, normal and his work bio was the last thing she had looked at. He was a manager in the project development area.

"You came directly from the office. Where is that?"

"You look lovely."

"Thank you."

"Andover & Associates. It's downtown."

She lifted her wineglass from the counter and took a sip. Good. "I'd never heard of it before you handed me your card."

"We do land development mostly."

"Is that why you want my land, to develop it?"

"Wouldn't you rather save the business talk until later?"

"No. I'd rather get it over with."

He shrugged. "We're contracting with the Wagner Company to develop several plots of land in the area adjacent to your own forty acres."

"Develop into what?"

"Private luxury resort."

"A resort with a big wall?" Mira thought for a minute. "Isn't the Wagner Group primarily big pharma? Why do they need a resort?"

"I don't know. Can't say."

She read his eyes. She wondered which one it was—don't know or can't say. "Isn't it pretty far from the city for that kind of development?"

"I know that they like their privacy. I suspect that's why they're building a tall wall around the resort."

Mira cocked her head to the side as she tried to imagine why anyone might need a luxury resort with a tall barrier. "That's not very encouraging to me," she said.

"Think of it this way. The Wagner Company is developing the area, whether you sell or not. The neighborhood won't stay the same as it is now."

Mira thought about her once-beautiful river and stellar view. She was beginning to realize that it was gone already. Mira lost her appetite. She couldn't help but think that the Wagner Company had some nefarious purpose. A resort welcomed people in. They didn't need privacy. They didn't need a wall. They were working hard to ruin it all. "I've changed my mind. I don't think I want to go out to dinner."

He prattled on for a bit trying to make her feel better about the sell. His words fell over each other in his rush to convince her, but she wasn't going to let him put pressure on her tonight.

"I need some time," she said. She still didn't know if

the sale of the land was the excuse for the date or the date was all about the sale of land.

She shook his hand politely and opened the door for him to leave. She was exhausted by the whole encounter, by the whole weekend. She dropped the dress to the floor and sat down limply on her bed.

Chapter 17 – *Mira* - Monday, April 27, 2026

Mira was running late for her first class on Monday, but she still took the time to drop off her specimens at the lab.

"Can I get a rush on it?" Mira asked.

"We don't usually do special requests," the receptionist said. Her young eyes met Mira's with optimism. Her smile was genuine. She seemed anxious to please.

Mira said, "It's really important."

The receptionist leaned forward and spoke in conspiratorial tones, "Come back at three o'clock. I'll see what I can do."

Mira leaned forward and whispered, "Thank you. I really appreciate it." She handed the receptionist her basket of jars of mud and mucky water.

She stopped at her car to watch the light play tricks with the treetops on the hills. There was a squirrel on the power line overhead, twitching his tail in her face. The sky was white and the air smelled clean.

The lab was about ten miles west of town. The road was narrow and winding. They had installed a few signal lights to slow the traffic, but the street was known to be perilous. She took it slow and easy, and so was considerably late when she arrived at school.

Just the same, she parked and walked to the west mall. It was a sunny, blue-sky day with a temperature in the low eighties. Halfway up the steps to the mall, with the traffic on the Drag roaring behind her, she spotted a wavy, brown bob and dark eyes black with kohl—Isa Vedkka.

She'd met Isa here on the mall. Their schedules matched in a way that had Isa and Mira buying coffee three times a week at the same time. At first, it was 'hi' or 'how you doing?' but soon the conversations grew. Mira could see that Isa was an artist. She usually wore two shirts, the top one covered in an assortment of paint splotches.

"You cut your hair. The purple ends are gone."

"Yes." It was time. "Don't you have class right about now?" Isa asked.

Mira shrugged.

"Three weeks to go and you're giving up?"

"It's been a tough few days."

"What happened?"

"At the land this weekend, my friend was bitten by a cottonmouth snake. I think the snake came to ground because the water in my river is polluted."

"Wow. That is a bad few days."

"Everything feels wrong and I'm not sure why. I feel the same as when my father died – like I've lost everything."

"There's always more to lose," Isa said.

Mira didn't find this very comforting, and so let the subject drop.

Isa dug into her backpack. After rooting around, she pulled out a battered and scratched canister. She popped the lid and blew a puff of air into Mira's face.

"Smells nice, doesn't it?"

"Floral." Mira decided this must be some kind of art experience that Isa had come up with. Mira's own backpack dug into her shoulder. She turned around and set it on the ledge behind her.

"I wish I had more," Isa said, "but I don't."

Mira didn't know why the white Camry caught her attention. Maybe it was the slow speed at which it passed. Students usually zipped down the street, nearly knocking over anyone in their path. But she did notice the car and it stuck with her.

"It's not even summer yet and it's so hot. Want to get an iced coffee?" Isa asked.

Mira was absurdly late, so she said, "Sure." She'd get notes from someone. She'd much rather chat with Isa.

Mira moved her backpack to a table near the coffee cart and then went to order an iced regular and an iced chai latte.

She didn't know Isa all that well. She didn't know what foods Isa liked best or what music she listened to. Isa had a boyfriend named Rory, but Mira had never met him. She knew that Isa understood Mira's commitment to being a lawyer. It was the same as Isa's commitment to art. Isa knew what it took to get up every day and make it to class. She understood how hard it was to study weeknights in lieu of having fun. Many mornings, Isa sat by the coffee cart and helped Mira study for her MPRE, a prerequisite test to taking the bar. Mira owed Isa. Mira liked Isa, yet Mira had never invited Isa to the land.

Her friends at the land lived in a different, separate world. That was part of the attraction—not mixing school with fun. That was part of the dilemma that she had been struggling with lately—how to leave behind the party life, live her professional life, but keep her party family.

Mira had gone home to study. About one-thirty in the afternoon, she closed her books and took a cool shower. She was anxious to find out what the lab knew. She left her apartment early, thinking she would wait if she arrived too soon at the lab. She packed her backpack and laptop and put them into the car.

Pulling away from her apartment, she saw the white

Camry. It pulled into traffic in front of her and passed her by.

She didn't see the car again until she was well out of town, on the twisting road that went through the hill country. Her pulse picked up. Her heart started to pound. She was definitely being followed. She picked up speed.

"Don't panic," she cautioned herself. "Don't slow down. Don't stop and don't panic." She inhaled deeply to steady her breathing. "Calm." When she felt more in control, she thought about her options. "Now what?"

On a tight curve, the white Camry raced up behind her. Mira watched him coming in her rearview mirror. He rushed closer until he smacked her rear bumper, jerking her head on her neck. He nudged her out of control. She skidded with her full force on the brakes. He pushed her toward a ditch, but her car stopped on the shoulder.

He took off, turning around up the road. He was going to come back. She backed up and took off in the opposite direction, but he was on her in a few seconds. It was going too fast. She would be dead before she had time to think. She had to think.

The white Camry looked new and in good condition. Her Chevy was old and needed a tune-up. She couldn't outrun him. She couldn't out maneuver him, but....

Fried Green Tomatoes. She slowed enough to let him pull beside her on the outside lane. He had on a ball cap and sunglasses. She couldn't make out his features, but he was definitely up to no good.

On her right was a hill. On his left, was a steady fifty-foot drop. He was taunting her, but she wasn't willing to play. As he began to ease ahead of her, she turned her front bumper hard into his right, front tire and pushed. She gave it the gas. Rubber burned as she pushed him off the road. He skidded half way down the slope, his tire shredded.

"Ha," she laughed. "Hope you have insurance."

She drove on about fifty yards, stopped and looked back. She was shaking, sweating and panting.

He got out of his car. He was shaking too. He looked unstable. He circled the Camry, yelling what she assumed were obscenities. She tried to make out more of his features, but couldn't. Now she understood why. He had on a dark facemask. She looked at his clothes, his walk, the way he was expressing his fit of anger. *Who was he?* She had no idea.

He saw her and stumble/ran toward her. What was wrong with him? Was he on drugs? Mira decided it was time to go.

Up the road, she stopped and called the police. They promised to be there within thirty minutes. She decided not to wait. She didn't want to find out what he wanted before the police arrived.

Mira turned off the main road onto a dirt drive before reaching the building. She opened an unlocked a gate, crossed a cattle grate and followed the drive until she could see the lab in the distance. She pulled off the road and drove over dirt pasture until the car was behind a stand of trees, no longer visible in almost any direction. She ran a half-mile toward the back of the building, watching the parking lot as best she could.

When she reached the lab, she walked around the outside and peeked in a few windows. She saw technicians working in one room. The rest of the building seemed empty. Things looked normal, so she went inside.

She went straight to the public restroom and threw some water on her face. She was still panting, maybe from her run, but likely from her panic. She gripped the sides of the wash basin and took a few deep breathes.

She sat in the formal reception area. A few cushioned chairs and standard issue prints hid the look of real work that went on behind the wall. Reception was quiet and empty.

A technician came through the door. He looked like he worked out and that made Mira smile. "Ms. Ashe," he said. "Will you come with me please?"

Mira stood up and followed him into a small, common use office just inside the lobby door. She felt relieved to be in a hidden space with a beefy man.

"Let me make certain I have this straight. You have a lagoon of limited size where there is a bad odor.

"Yes. That's right."

"Anything else?"

"It's green," Mira said. "Shamrock green."

"And this land isn't developed. It's been in private ownership for at least five years."

"Yes, but it wasn't developed, even before me." She paused for a minute. "There is construction going on across the river."

"What kind?"

"Buildings—like houses. And a wall."

"There's no chemical plant or oil refinery nearby."

"No."

"What about big agriculture? Large farms?"

"Some farming. None I'd call big."

"Do you burn waste?"

"No. We generally only use the land on weekends. On Sundays, we recycle or compost what we can. Anything left, we pack up and take it to the dumpster at a store nearby."

"You have evidence of hydrogen sulfide gas—H2S."

"Hydrogen sulfide? Is it toxic to humans?"

"It can be. It depends on the amount and length of

exposure. Doses can be quite dangerous if you have high levels of H2S or are exposed over a long period of time." He looked at her. "It shouldn't be in the area of the river."

"Like the cottonmouth?"

"What?"

"Never mind."

He pointed to her mud sample. "You can see oil. See?" He rubbed the slick substance between his fingers.

"This is sour crude oil. It emits the H2S. This can lead to serious health problems."

"Like what?" Mira thought of her father, suddenly afraid he had something to do with this. "Breathing?"

"Exactly. Heart and lungs."

Mira didn't know it was possible for her heart to beat any faster. She was beginning to get light-headed. "Where does it come from?" she asked.

"It's a byproduct of combustion processing. Usually I would think from an oil refinery."

"Okay. "

"And there was also something else in the mix. Algae. The green is algae blooms. There is a problem in lakes and ocean shorelines that has significantly increased in the last fifty years. It's called eutrophication or hypoxic dead zones."

"Well that sounds horrible."

"It is. Chemicals like nitrogen, phosphorous or in this case hydrogen sulfide fertilize blooms of toxic algae. It grows out of control, helped along by the triple-digit weather we've been experiencing. The algae covers the water so light and air can't get through. It consumes all the oxygen."

"So, the fish suffocated?"

"Exactly, " he said. "The closest dead zone I know about is in the Gulf of Mexico. It runs about 7,000 square miles along the shoreline close to the mouth of the Mississippi."

"What caused that dead zone?"

"Well, in the Gulf, it's caused by the crap that people dump into the Mississippi from Montana, Minnesota, Iowa on south. Things like fertilizers from farms or human waste."

"That can't be it for my land, can it?"

"I suppose it's possible. There has been a lot of flooding to the North of us, resulting in erosion and run-off, but my guess is that somebody has been dumping on your property."

"I don't know what to do. What would you do?"

"If it were me, I'd contact the authorities: police and get an investigation going."

"Thanks," she said. She took her report, left by the back door and hiked the half mile to her car. She saw no signs of the white Camry or any other suspicious activity.

Chapter 18 – *Mira* - Monday, April 27, 2026

After leaving the lab, Mira drove to the closest police station. She met with Officer Jillian Hyatt, a big-boned woman, as her mother called people who were large but not heavy, who looked to be in her mid-twenties. Officer Hyatt took Mira's statement and followed her out to the stretch of highway where she was run off the road. The Camry was gone. Mira guessed that she shouldn't have been surprised. There were some muddy tracks and rubber marks on the road, but beyond that there was little to verify her story. The blood rushed from Mira's head and she struggled to stay on her feet.

The officer took her elbow to steady her.

"So, what happens now?" Mira asked.

"I'm sorry, but there's not much I can do. There's not enough evidence of a crime."

"Someone tried to run me off the road. Right here." Mira's terror was rising again.

"I'm sorry, but...."

Mira's voice went up in pitch and volume. "And that's not the only suspicious thing that has happened lately."

"What do you mean?" The officer looked attentive and concerned.

"There was a venomous snake in my bed." Mira said. "It bit my friend. They say it was because of the poisoned water."

"Poisoned water?"

"That's where I was going. To the lab that tested the water." Mira waved her copy of the report and the officer took a photo of it. "The poisonous snake came from the poisoned water."

"Could be that someone is trying to scare you."
"Well, it's working," Mira said.

Mira didn't bother to go home. She found a branch for her bank that was close to the last place she was seen–the crash on the highway, and drew out three thousand dollars. She pulled the SIM card from her cell phone and drove across town.

She checked into a cheap motel and paid for a day up front with cash. No one questioned her or asked for identification or a credit card. Mira assumed that related to the half dozen hookers on the corner.

She pulled out everything in her car: her books and laptop, a few items of clothing she had thrown into a bag for the weekend. Miles' laundry and softball gear were also in her car. She got those out as well.

When the car was empty, she drove it a mile down the street and left it for repairs. The front bumper had been nearly dragging the ground and the fender needed to be pounded out. She also requested that tune-up she had been needing for a while. She wanted her car running well. They locked the car in the garage overnight planning to fix it in the morning. She rented a wreck from the mechanic, a thirteen-year-old Honda Civic with a mismatched doors, and drove it back to the motel. She felt vulnerable and alone.

In her motel room, she sat on the bed propped up against the wall with both pillows. There was an odor, so she pulled the sheets and pillowcases off the bed.

She was hiding out. She paced the limited space and wondered at it. She surveyed her belongings, thinking about their value in a life and death situation. She got up and got Miles' bat and held it close to her chest.

She thought about changing the color of her hair. Isn't that what people do when hiding out, change their hair, change their look? She took a shower, borrowed one of Miles' tee shirts and then settled for a braid and Miles' ball cap.

Mira picked up the dirty sheets and threw them into the laundry basket. She loaded the dirty clothes from her bag and Miles' discarded laundry into his basket and walked around the corner to the motel's laundry room. She started to sort whites from colors, but ended by intermingling all of Miles' clothes with all of her own. She wanted to cry, but resolved not to. She had to be hard, just as she should be when hiding out.

While the clothes washed, Mira walked a few blocks to a little park. She stood behind a tree, put the SIM card in and turned on her cell phone. Mira selected a contact on her list.

"Hello," Andee's voice came over the line. She sounded off, hazy somehow.

"Hi. It's me. I wanted to check to see how Jimmy Rey is today."

"His snake bite is fine, but we've both picked up that flu bug that's going around. Have you seen it on the news? Jimmy Rey was easy pickings with his compromised immune system and I was easy pickings from him."

"Oh no," Mira said. She felt her level of panic ratchet up. She couldn't help but remember the COVID epidemic. Even the mildest flu outbreak set her on edge. "I'll come over and make you some chicken soup."

"No. Stay away. You don't need this."

Mira sat down hard under her tree.

"What's going on with you?" Andee said. "You seem off?"

"Bad people, I think."

"Bad people? You don't believe in bad people," Andee said.

"I've recently had to revise some of my more naïve ideas, but I'm not going to ruin the trust I feel in the people that I care most about."

"You're scaring me."

"I'm scaring myself," Mira said. Mira brought her up to date.

"So, someone tried to run you off the road," Andee said with alarm in her voice. "On purpose."

"There's no doubt in my mind," Mira said, although there was some doubt in her mind.

"What's your plan? You always have a plan."

"Nothing is worth putting my friends or myself in harm's way. My plan is to give him whatever he wants."

"Call the police Mira. I'm worried about you." Andee sighed in exasperation.

"I have. Don't worry about me. I'm hiding out. Take care of you," Mira said.

Andee said, "Finish school. Get a job. Live your life."

"Okay. I'll call you later to see if you've changed your mind about the soup." She hung up. Mira fiddled with her phone, checked her messages.

"Hi," Jayson's voice said. "I wanted to say that I hope to see you again-whatever you decide."

"Yeah right," she talked back to the phone.

She selected the second message. "Mira. It's your Sweetie," Riley said. "I'm looking for you. Call me."

"Mira, Hi. This is Miles–Miles Lynton. I'm playing softball tomorrow. I could use my glove, ball and bat. I went out to the land. They weren't there." He stammered a bit. "Maybe you'd like to join us?"

Good guys and bad guys. Who was who? What did they want? Her head competed with her heart.

Mira did have to return Miles' belongings. How could Miles play ball without his equipment? Her instinct was to trust him. She believed with every fiber of her being that she could, but she wasn't stupid. She knew instincts could be wrong.

When she got back to her room, she sorted the clean clothes into his and hers, putting hers into a neat pile and his back into the laundry basket. She gave the mattress a little whiff and decided it was okay. She redressed the bed with the clean sheets.

She paced the room, thinking.

She pulled out a legal pad from her backpack and looked at the top sheet in front of her. There were some notes about torts. She folded over the used pages and secured them to the cardboard backing with a paperclip.

She sat on the bed, propped against the wall. On the top of the blank page, she wrote a question. She stared at the even lines and blank rows under the question, "Who is not what they seem?" She willed an answer to come to her. She stared into space for an hour, waiting for her thoughts to clear. It wasn't happening. It didn't make sense. Nothing fit together. She had to start eliminating some of her suspects—or nailing them. She'd start with the man she knew best. Mira grabbed the keys for her rented car and went out the door.

Chapter 19 - *Mira* - Monday – April 27, 2026

Riley was the logical place to start her investigation. She had known him the longest. Mira drove to Riley's house, but he wasn't at home. She had one other idea for where to find him.

There were mostly pickup trucks in the parking lot. Riley's black mustang convertible stood out.

It was loud when she walked in the door with a lot of conflicting noise: carnival music, sounds like distant thunder, bells and children yelling. It wasn't as crowded as she expected. She looked around. Online video games had taken away most of the arcade business.

Most of the people there were under the age of twelve. Riley was playing air hockey with a ten-year-old boy. Several other boys stood around watching. Riley had a cup full of tokens sitting next to him. The boys would lift one every now and then and he would pretend not to notice. Mira imagined that this is how Riley gained their acceptance.

Mira looked at the pinball screen closest to her. The top-scoring player was listed as RM. The number was in the thousands. He hung out here a lot.

When she thought about it, she actually knew a lot about Riley. He had been hanging around for over a year. Riley had had a birthday a month ago. He was thirty. He did fairly well at selling real estate. He was attractive, cute really, and had an easy nature, but he was persistent like a willful child who wanted something badly. The same tenacity made him good at volleyball and likely air hockey as well. He never gave up.

His concentration on his game was total. He leaned into his movements, standing with one hand behind his back. He watched the puck. It wasn't until it was over that he noticed her standing there. He smiled in an unguarded manner.

"Hey Mira. I've never seen you here before."

"I've never been. I was looking for you."

The boys snickered and taunted.

"Me?" He tilted his head, like he was having trouble understanding.

"I wanted to talk about your offer."

"Oh." He smiled. "Okay."

"Is there someplace a little quieter?"

He waved his hand in a wide sweep. "There isn't any place quiet around here. Maybe over there." He pointed to an alcove where tables and chairs were reserved for children's birthday parties. "No one is using it." Riley picked up his tokens and slipped into the crowd as he called back to her, "I'll meet you there."

Mira walked over and sat at a table covered in black and white checkered contact paper. It was slick and tacky to the touch.

In a minute, he bounded up. "I won this for you in the Gift Box over there." Riley pointed to a machine. It had key chains, little cars, and one nice watch, each in their own gift box. The player picked up the box with a magnet if they were lucky. Mira was impressed. She had never been able to snag anything in one of those machines.

Riley opened the box he brought to her, lifted her hand and slipped a cheap metal ring with an adjustable band and a huge glass stone on her left ring finger.

"Why do you want to marry me?" She cautioned, "Don't say you love me because I don't believe that."

"What? No. That's not true."

"Tell me a different story." She waited for him to talk. "Tell me the truth, please." She saw his face yield from surrender.

"Your father bought forty prime acres, bound to be worth exponentially more as the city encroaches, especially since it's the best property around that new development. When he died, he willed the land to his only living relative."

"This I know," Mira said.

"He hired a good friend, Alonzo Rossi, to manage the property for his daughter."

"Also know."

"When Andover & Associates became interested, I became interested too. They're a big land development company. Major contracts. Getting in on the ground floor with them would be huge for me."

"You never planned to buy the land. You don't have the money," Mira speculated. "What then?" When he didn't answer, she did it for him, "You wanted to marry it."

"No! I wanted to be the agent of record. That's all. I wanted us to be together for other reasons—romantic reasons."

Riley and Mira sat quietly in the chaos for another few seconds. The truth, Mira decided.

"I still think we should get married. I want to."

Mira didn't reply. Mira thought of Riley like a little brother. She had no interest in marrying him.

"You're the most important person in my life," Riley said.

"Someone tried to run me off the road today."

"On purpose?" Riley's mouth fell open in surprise. He looked concerned and unhappy.

Mira stood up to leave. She folded his glass diamond into his palm. His expression told her all she needed to know.

Chapter 20 – *Mira* – Tuesday, April 28, 2026

Mira met Miles at the ballpark at three o'clock in the afternoon. When she first arrived, it was lightly raining–a mist really, but there was a no umbrella rule. Mira had only two things to wear, shorts and the top she had worn to school last Friday and the tee-shirt and shorts she wore to the land. She had opted for the Friday shorts. It was cooler than on Friday, cloudy and damp. She wasn't dressed for the weather.

Miles was playing first base. He looked lean and taut. She watched his movements, his gestures and felt sick at suspecting him.

He played ball like it was the most important activity in the world. He was serious, but she could see that he was also a good teammate. He didn't lose his temper when a call went against him or a player made a critical mistake. He only yelled encouragement.

"Are you Mira?" A petite woman with waist-length brown hair stood in front of her, smiling. "I'm Tina." She pointed to the pitcher. "I'm Cal's wife." Tina took Miles' ball, bat and glove handed them to a team member who stood on the sidelines. "I've been instructed to take good care of you. May I join you?"

"I'd like that."

They took seats in the stands among a small crowd on damp bleachers with moisture swirling around her arms and face.

"Dreary day, isn't it? Are you cold?" She spread a light cotton blanket over Mira's bare legs.

"So who gets to play in a softball league that meets on

weekdays?" Mira asked.

"College students, people that work a four-day work week, people who can make their own hours, and people who are willing to sneak out early," Tina said.

"Which are you?"

"Cal and I operate a private school. Kids go home at three o'clock, so basically we sneak out early."

"Have you known Miles for long?" Mira asked.

"Only about six days, but he's great."

"Is he?" She tried to keep her tone light. "Six days isn't very long."

"How long does it take to recognize good people?" Tina asked.

Mira watched Miles, lost in her own thoughts for a few minutes. Tina spoke to her, pulling her back. She was shivering. "What?" she asked.

"I'm supposed to invite you to join us for beer and pizza after the game. It's tradition."

"I don't know."

"You have to. Cal and Miles will both kill me if you say no."

Kill me. The words echoed in her mind. She tried to hold her knees still without success.

"You're still cold," Tina said.

"No. I'm okay." She looked at the sweet, gentle face of Tina.

"I just love Miles to death," Tina said.

To death, she heard.

"He hasn't talked about anything else since we got here. If I weren't married, I'd be jealous."

The sun came out, shined into Mira's eyes over first base and the world lit up with color. The infield grass was so green. She was struck with the most intense sense of déjà vu as she remembered the sunny day when her father told her he was dying.

Dad didn't help with her homework. He didn't teach her how to mow the lawn or change the oil in a car. He didn't teach her about hard work or handling money. These things she learned on her own. He taught her about wishing for things she did not have. He taught her about dreaming. She allowed a single tear to slip down her damp cheek. The land is what he cared about and the wealth it might one day bring her. That was her inheritance. His dreams for her.

"I wouldn't want to get you in trouble," Mira said. "I guess I'll have to come with you for a beer."

Unbidden, her thoughts were drawn back to that day in the ballpark. Before she really started to listen, her father had told a story from his past. Her grandmother had told her father and his brothers for years that she was saving something special for them when she died. In the days before her death, she laid out four little packages. After the service, each of the brothers opened the package with their name on it. Inside each was a small, white Christening gown. The stitch work was intricate and the embroidery beautiful. Each gown held the smell of the ointment she put on her hands to warm the stiffness and allow her to do the tiny piecework.

"None of us wanted an infant's christening gown," he had said. "We were teenagers, but it was the most valuable thing she thought she had, so I kept it. At least, I can leave you something valuable, something you can take to the bank one day."

Mira wondered what had happened to her father's beautiful christening gown made with love by her grandmother.

"Do I get the christening gown too?" she'd had asked.

"Yeah. If I can find it. You can have that too," her

father had said.

"Could you excuse me for a minute," Mira told Tina. She climbed out of the bleachers and moved out of view. She wiped the tears as they fell freely down her face. Her father always had some impractical scheme. Nothing good ever came of them. The land wasn't a promise of future money to her. Her father had given the land to her because he cared about her in his own way. It was the only way he knew how to tell her he loved her.

"Are you all right?" Tina had followed her down.

"Did you ever have a day that changed your whole life?" Mira looked out at the field. The light shifted as clouds moved across the sky. The players switched for the start of a new inning.

"Huh?" Tina asked.

"I'm fine." And she knew she would be.

After the game, they went to a pizza place with a real brick oven. The oven added warmth and a soft red glow to the dining room. A large-screen television filled a wall on one side and the bar ran the length of another. From her seat at the table, Mira could see the whole long room. She glanced around nervously.

"Do you want to get a pitcher?" Cal said.

"I better not," Mira said.

"Not that house beer," Tina said.

When the pitcher arrived and four glasses, Cal filled three glasses, and then waited for her go-ahead. She relented and nodded.

After he poured her a second glass of beer, she relaxed. The conversation was smooth and had the camaraderie of old friends. Cal was funny; Tina was smart; and Miles still made her pulse beat faster.

One pitcher of beer turned into two. One pizza turned into two. Miles ate a discarded crust of her slice of pizza.

"I have a question for you?" Mira asked Miles.

He waited for her to go on.

"Why are you interested in me?"

He smoothed a stray hair away from her eyes and touched her cheek. "You're smart, pretty, but it's more." His hand fell from her face to cover her hand.

"Do you want to buy or steal my land by the river?"

He flinched in surprise. "No. Why would I?"

"The land could be valuable."

"It's pleasant out there, but I'm only here temporarily. I'm on assignment from work. I live in D.C. At least for now."

She waited for another answer.

"Plus, it's too far out of town for me. You spend every weekend out there," he said. "I play in this softball league. The games are mostly on the weekends. Plus, I use my days off to practice and play the game. I was hoping to share that with you, but I can't if you're out on the land."

"Andover & Associates is building a private luxury resort there."

"What's this all about?"

"You tell me."

He seemed at a loss for what to say. He settled on, "It's a shame to build over such an attractive area."

"How long?" she asked. "You said your stay is temporary."

"Don't know. Days, Weeks, Months. Until the job is done."

"What job?"

He didn't answer, and so she knew that was the right question to ask.

She excused herself and went to the bathroom. Before returning to the table, she looked at her party. She couldn't see Cal's face from where she stood, only his broad shoulders and the back of his short hair. His hands waved in the air. He was telling a story. Tina touched Miles' back, but not in a way that made her jealous. It was a friendly gesture. Miles was laughing, his gray eyes bright. His long fingers circled his glass of beer. The hands of an artist like her friend Isa, she thought. She didn't know what Miles did for a living. She had never asked and he had never told. He could be an artist for all she knew. *A government artist,* she thought.

Cal and Tina stood to leave. They approached her and gave her a hug like long-lost friends.

"Looks like rain again. We're gonna take off. Hope we see you again soon."

"Me too," Mira said. She looked back at Miles. He put his credit card on the bill. Apparently, he was paying.

Shouting and clapping drew her attention in the direction of the big screen T.V. The bar was crowded, mostly with men in their twenties or thirties watching a game. They cheered loudly and slapped each other.

One man caught her eye. He didn't' fit. He saw her and held up his beer in a small salute. Mira could see the ends of his salt and pepper hair peeking from under his gimmie cap.

Mira heard a dull tapping. She looked out the window. It was a storm. She hoped Cal and Tina had made it to their car. Hail the size of peas battered the windows. It was a quick storm, over as she watched. The icy particles turned to rain.

Miles came up behind Mira and that made her jump.

"You okay?" he asked.

She nodded.

"Would you like another drink?

"No. Thanks."

A man with salt and pepper hair made his way toward

them.

"This is Detective Walt Liskin with the Austin police," Miles said. "Miles sat on a stool at the bar. "Will you sit for a while? I want to tell you about my father."

Part II

Chapter 21 – *Miles* - March 2003

Seven-year-old Miles got up before the sun. He pulled on his jeans and a Lenny Kravitz tee-shirt. He picked up the flannel shirt he had worn the day before. He wanted to button it up, but on his third try without getting it right, he gave up. He grabbed his new sneakers.

"Mom," he yelled.

Even though Miles was not allowed to wake her before the sun was shining, he knew on this day she would already be up.

"Not those," she said. Mom sat on the sofa in her fuzzy bathrobe cuddling a cup of herbal tea. "Get your high-top boots."

"I want to show him my new shoes," Miles said. They were blue and had Velcro.

"You can show him, but you need to wear something sturdier. Dad will want you to wear the right shoes for the hike-ones you don't mind getting muddy. And grab a cap."

"Which one?"

"Any one. Your favorite."

Miles ran to his room and found his good boots for hiking and a ball cap. Back in the living room, Mom helped him put on the boots and tie them right.

"How many minutes before Dad gets here?"

"I don't know, sweetie."

Dad worked at a refinery near the Galveston beach every night but one. It was more than three hours away, so he stayed there with some other men. No women or children, so Mom and Miles couldn't stay with him.

"Dad worked until two o'clock in the morning, so he needs to get a few hours of sleep before he drives home to us for the weekend," Mom said.

"But when will he be here?" Miles repeated.

"Maybe he had to work overtime. Maybe he overslept because he was too tired. I don't

know what time he left Texas City, so I can't tell you what time he will be home."

Miles pulled on the sash of Mom's fuzzy robe.

"Let's make breakfast," she said. "Maybe Dad will be here to eat with us when it's ready. What do you want?"

"Dad likes pancakes."

"Sometimes, but Dad also likes eggs."

Miles made a face.

"How about we make both?" Mom said. "Will you help me?"

Miles nodded.

"Get the Bisquick," she said.

Mom went into her bedroom to put on her clothes. Miles could hear her talking on the phone.

"We're making pancakes. What's your ETA?"

"I want to talk," Miles said.

"Sorry Sweetie, he didn't answer. He must be driving, so I left him a message."

"Can I leave a message?"

"Sure." Mom dialed the number and handed Miles the phone.

"Hi Dad. Come home so we can go before it gets too hot." That was something his dad said all the time. They should go early before it gets too hot.

Mid-morning, Miles was curled into Mom's lap. She stroked his hair away from his moist eyes.

The uneaten pancakes were stacked on a plate on the kitchen island. One plate filled with food that Mom had encouraged Miles to eat sat hardly touched on the table.

"Can we call Dad again?"

"I don't think he's answering," Mom said. "Tell you what? Why don't you play for a while and I'll call his work and try to find out what time he left? Okay?"

Miles climbed off her lap, but didn't pick up any of his toys. He watched Mom as she retrieved the cordless phone and dialed.

"Hi. This is Geri Lynton. I was expecting my husband, Henry, home this morning, but he hasn't arrived."

Someone yelled. "Hey Lonny, you seen Henry Lynton?" He spoke into the phone. "We haven't seen him, but I'll take a look around. Give me your number and I'll call you back."

Mom started to cry even before the phone began to ring, so Miles began to cry too. She was gagging as she answered the call.

"I'm sorry, Ma'am. We think he left after his shift on Thursday night."

"What!? When?"

"Nobody here's seen him since Thursday."

"Did he say where he was going? Did he have Friday night off?"

You should call the supervisor, Ma'am."

Mom got a pad and wrote down a name and phone number.

She sat still and quiet for a few minutes. Then she picked up the phone again and called Josh's mom.

"Can Miles come play with Josh today?"

"No." Miles whined. "I want to wait for Dad."

She shushed him. "I'll come get you as soon as Dad is home. I promise." She turned back to the phone, and Mrs. Taylor said she was on her way over to get him.

Mrs. Taylor arrived inside five minutes, still wearing a

tee-shirt she had slept in and sweat pants.

Josh was talking to Miles, but he wasn't listening like a good friend. He was trying to hear Mrs. Taylor as she talked in a low voice.

"What will you do?" Mrs. Taylor said.

"I'm going to make calls."

"Who will you call?"

"Everyone," Mom said. "I thought I'd start with the highway patrol, hospitals and morgues."

Mrs. Taylor shuffled Josh and Miles out the door as Mom picked up the pad with the phone number they had given her at work.

Dad was still not home by the end of the day. Miles eyes hurt and his nose was stuffy. Mom sat by his bed, but he couldn't fall asleep, so she climbed into bed with him and held him in her arms. Soon, they were both crying for Daddy. When Mom climbed out of the bed, he was still awake. She turned on his bunny nightlight lamp. He kept his eyes closed and lay still in the dark as she kissed his forehead.

Mom left his bedroom door open. He could see her working on the computer. The phone rang.

"Hello," she said. He held his breath.

"No. He went down hard, but he's in bed."

Mom listened for a long time.

"I know. I know, Mom." His mom put her phone on speaker, so Miles could hear Grandma too.

"What are you doing now?" Grandma asked.

"I'm doing some Internet searches. I started out with a search on "what do you do when your husband doesn't come home?" All the results were about philandering. You don't think…"

"I do not," Grandma said, "and neither should you."

Miles thought about that word "philandering." He

didn't know it or what it meant, but it sounded bad.

"I'm sure that's what all these angry Internet women thought too. They complain about the surprise, the lack of common courtesy and respect."

"Stop that."

"I want to be angry. I want him to come home with some stupid excuse so I can be angry, because any other alternative is too horrid."

"Maybe his car broke down."

"And his phone too?" Neither spoke for a minute.

Miles got out of bed. He grabbed his Teddy from the toy bin where he had left it a long time ago. He lay down on the floor close to the door where he could hear better.

"And then," Mom continued, "I looked up 'missing loved one.' Its results were all about death."

"I know you must have, but did you check hospitals?"

"And morgues too."

"Have you called the police?"

"They say that they won't do anything for forty-eight hours. Adults have a right to disappear. I'm going to go camp on their doorstep in the morning."

Miles got up. He went to her. "I'm coming too."

"Of course you are, sweetie."

Chapter 22 – *Walt* - March 2003

From his new desk in the bullpen of the Austin Police Department, Walt Liskin watched the woman walk into the common area. She was petite with what appeared to be natural blonde hair and wet blue eyes. She lugged a huge bag over her shoulder, likely with the necessities of caring for a small boy. Her little son held her hand with one of his. In his other hand, he clutched some papers. He held his head high like a tiny man.

"My husband is missing," she said to Walt, "and don't even go through the list of excuses that newbie policeman gave me. He has not run away or gone catting around. He is not on a merchant ship or at a new job. It doesn't matter what that report he wrote says. My husband is missing."

"What's your name ?" Walt asked as he shifted through active folders.

"Mrs. Geraldine Lynton. People call me Geri." Geri sat down in one of his guest chairs and Miles sat next to her.

Just the same, Walt gave the report an eyeball. "Tell me what happened?" he said.

"Henry. His name is Henry Lynton. He was working for Origin Oil Refinery in Texas City. Do you know it?"

Walt shook his head.

"It's just mainland of Galveston Island. They were fighting a deadline and needed extra help, so they brought on a handful of guys."

"Like contractors?"

"More like hard-working, hard-on-luck types. Henry was unemployed. Oil money is good and the work was promised for six months."

"And time is up? Your husband didn't come home?"

"No. It's only been three months. But he called every night—just to say hi and see how we were doing. He'd sing a little song to Miles before Henry started his night shift at the refinery. Then last Thursday—nothing. I haven't heard from him in four days." Her eyes welled again. "It's just not like him."

"Have you tried calling him?" Walt asked.

"Of course. Over and over. The night manager is new. He says Henry's not there. He says that he never even met Henry, but the guys he worked with say he disappeared on Thursday night."

"How many on the crew?"

"They hired fifteen extra guys."

"Have you tried calling them or the wives of any of the others?"

Geri lowered her head in a sorrowful shake. "The supervisor won't tell me their names. Says that's private."

"Did your husband mention anyone by name? Was there anyone he didn't get along with?"

"We didn't talk about things like that. We talked about Miles and what to do when the landlord came around again."

Walt thought that the officer who took the original statement was a lazy slob. To him, this seemed worth at least a few calls. "Give me the number, okay?"

Geri looked at Miles who handed over the paper he was holding. "Here's all I know."

"Thank you, young man." Walt acknowledged Miles grown up role in the event.

It was a pitiful bit of parchment. The name and address of the oil company, their main number in Houston, email, website and the local number in Texas City.

"The men were housed in trailers at the site. Henry

said bunkbeds."

"Adult men, away from their families, likely beer or other alcohol, in a tiny trailer. That doesn't sound good."

"Multiple trailers. Four people each: two people on the day shift and two on the night shift. Henry said that none of them did much more than sleep there. There was a TV and a little kitchenette, but they tended to prefer to go to the movies or to eat out. Henry didn't tell me about any fights."

But would he, Walt wondered. Walt dialed the local number and got no answer. He then tried the main number. When a receptionist picked up, he asked for the head of personnel.

"Hey there, this is Detective Walter Liskin with Austin P.D. I've got a few questions." His call was forwarded. "And who are you?" he asked. "The HR manager," he repeated for Geri's benefit. "One of your hires, a Mr. Henry Lynton, hasn't been in touch with his family in..." He lifted his eyes to Geri.

"Four days," she whispered."

Walt didn't finish the sentence, instead going a new way. "Mrs. Lynton was expecting him this weekend and he didn't show. She is very concerned."

Walt looked at young Miles. He didn't think it was normal for a child so young to be so silent and watchful, but Miles was taking in everything. He was a cute kid with downy white hair that would likely look much the same at seven and ninety-seven. He had enormous steel-gray eyes that followed Walt wherever he went.

"Really," Walt said into the phone when the HR guy told him that two men had disappeared in one night. "Two men?" he repeated.

Mrs. Lynton punched the speaker button on his phone so that she and her son could listen in. He didn't stop her.

"The night manager said they got a better offer," the HR guy said.

"What's the night manager's name," asked Walt.

"Last week it was Lonny Rossi. He said that the guys just up and left.

Walt scribbled a note. "Lonny is that short for something? Laurence?"

"Says here it was Alonzo," the HR guy said, with a 'z'. "Couple days later, he up and left too. There were some rumors."

"What kind of rumors?" Walt asked.

"That he got fired, not quit, but that's not true. No one was worried about those men at first—not until I got some anxious calls from a concerned wife."

"I'm gonna need all you got on the other missing man and a list of the names of the four contractors who shared that trailer and their contact info," he said.

"I'm not sure..." the HR guy started.

Walt cut in. "Look. Right now, this is your problem. You give me that info and it becomes mine. Yeah?"

"Yeah," the guy agreed. "Where should I send it?"

Walt gave him the information.

When the email arrived, Walt called the other wife, Helena Boskova. She didn't know a thing and hadn't heard from her husband, Eitan, in the last four days, but she hadn't expected him to call, both enjoying a break from each other.

There were lots of things that Walt hated about being a cop. Being inside the dingy common room done out in shades of gray doing paperwork was the second worst of them. The worst was working a case with no clues that seemed to offer little chance of justice.

Two men. Both missing. Only one mother and son seemed to care.

Walt watched as Geri dug into her big bag. She held out a coloring book to Miles, but he wasn't taking it. Instead, he continued to watch them.

Geri dug in her purse and handed some more papers to Miles.

"What've you got there?" Walt asked Miles.

Geri answered. "I gathered our last three months of phone and credit card bills. I thought they might help."

"Can I see?" he asked Miles and Miles handed them over. In a cursory glance, he didn't see anything interesting.

"Miles and I are going to the beach tomorrow," she said.

"You asked for our help. Let me investigate," Walt replied.

"I know him better than you. I might see something you would miss. Plus, I have ideas of my own."

"Like what kind of ideas?"

"Like looking for his car."

"You're right." Walt looked in the file and shook his head. "I need to put out an APB. What kind of car is it?"

"It's a Nissan Maxima, mostly dark blue.

"Mostly?"

"The rest is rust. About 80,000 miles, but it still runs. That's why we got it."

"I'll need the license plate number," Walt said. He wondered about Boskova's car. He'd have to call back his wife for that plate number as well.

Geri pulled out another bit of note paper passing it to Miles. Miles set it on Walt's desk.

"You don't have to search for the car. I can ask every cop in the state to be on the lookout for it."

Geri stared at him. "Thanks," she said as she stood to leave. Miles stared at him for a moment longer before he followed.

Next morning, Walt got into his car and went for a long drive. He didn't know, but he expected he might see Geri and her little son at his destination.

Chapter 23 – *Walt* - March 2003

Walt rolled down the window of his police car. From a distance, the Origin Oil Refinery was a lot of tall, smoky stacks—a cancer-causing factory. The hot, afternoon air smelled foul. He held his breath as he got out of the car.

He walked around the parking lot near a gate in front of the building. He talked to people and held up the driver's license photo of Henry Lynton.

"I'd like to talk to the two men who were sharing the trailer," Walt said when the guy in charge approached him.

"They're workin'," said the day manager. "You can't come in."

Walt spotted Geri and Miles getting out of her car. Miles gave him a big wave and he waved back. Miles and his mom creep forward until they were within listening distance.

"Five minutes," Walt said to the day manager.

The day manager looked uncertain. "Just you," he finally said and pointed to a security guard to go with Walt. Walt and the guard went one way and the day manager went another. A final guard stayed with Geri and Miles.

Inside was a huge, Tinker Toy network of pipes. All around him were men wearing yellow jumpsuits with reflective tape across the chest and around the arms.

His escort handed him a dirty helmet that had a slimy feel and an odor. Walt put it on his head without hesitating or making a face. "So, how's it work here?" he asked.

"Crude gets shipped in. We heat it up and remove

impurities, and then we add some stuff and make fuel."

"Well, that is succinct," Walt said about the man's short description. "Did you know Henry Lynton?"

"What color is he?"

Walt was thrown by the question. "White," he said tentatively.

"There is no white. Only yellow, red and blue."

"He was contract work."

"Orange then." Walt noted that orange was not yellow, red or blue, unless you mixed a couple of them together.

"This is Dac and Tiny Tim." His escort walked a few steps off.

"I'm looking for the men who shared the trailer with Henry Lynton and Eitan Boskova. Is that you?"

Tiny nodded his head.

Walt decided to jump to the heart of the matter. "Do you know where they are?"

"Naw. We hardly ever saw 'em even when they was working," Dac said. "Different shifts."

"When was the last time you recall?"

"Maybe Wednesday at change-over. Eitan had made some kind of goop for dinner and said we could finish it off."

"Did you?"

"Yeah," Tiny said. "It was pretty good."

"Any idea where they went?"

Both men looked at him, saying nothing.

"Thanks anyway."

When Walt came back, Miles was yelling at men as they went through the gate. "Hey. Where's my dad?" That made the men walk faster.

"I'd like to see the trailer where the two missing men were housed," Walt told a security guard.

"You can't."

"I can get a warrant by tomorrow." This was likely a ruse as he would have to get the local police involved and that would take time.

"It's not that. It's gone. Was gone the same night the guys left. Management will tell you otherwise, but that's the truth of it."

Walt and the guard walked over to the spot for the trailers. There was a big hole in the space where the last trailer would have been. Small, round stains made it look like something had spilled in the dirt. Walt pulled a black light from his pocket and turned it on. Nothing happened. No blood. Still, he gathered a small amount and put it in an evidence bag.

Walt turned and saw a brand, spanking new temporary building with two padlocks on it. "What's in there?" Walt asked. "Dangerous stuff?"

"Chemicals used in the oil refinery. Didn't use to be locked up. Just started doin' that."

"Did something happen? he asked.

"Not that I know of."

"Can I see?" Walt asked.

"No," the guard said and changed the subject. "Don't know where that trailer got to. Had to get a motel room for the day shift. The trailer guys wouldn't rent Origin another one. Had to buy the missing one. Management was not happy about that."

"And Lynton's stuff?" Walt asked.

"Wherever that trailer is."

Geri had inched closer. She and Miles stood in the parking lot on the opposite side of the fence. "And his car? Where's Henry's car?"

"Car's not here," the guard said.

Walt turned to her and asked, "Does your car have a trailer hitch?"

"No, it does not. It's not a powerful car."

"The other guy's car is still here. Your man could have driven the trailer hooked up to something."

So, Walt tramped over to take a look at Eitan Boskova's Ford Focus three-door hatchback.

"Well, this is a piece of junk," Walt said.

The guard nodded. "Two men—hard on their luck."

"I'll have someone come to tow this off."

Chapter 24 – *Walt* - March 2003

Back at the cars, Miles asked, "Are we going to the beach now?" He had a swim ring, a blue pail and a yellow shovel in the back seat that he pulled out to show Walt.

"We're going to make sandwiches on the island. A picnic." Geri said. "Want to come?" she asked Walt.

"Sure," he replied. He followed Geri's car beyond the Houston traffic and over the bridge to Galveston Island.

They drove down the seawall to the end of the island and back. They stopped at Stewart Beach.

"I come here with my family," Geri said. "This beach has bathrooms and a play area for kids."

They unpacked her car. She brought the makings for sandwiches, water and snacks to a picnic table. The three of them took off their shoes and walked down to the surf. The sun beat down on the sand blinding them and the surf rolled gently over thirty toes. Seaweed and trash had been plowed and was pushed into a hill near dunes covered in grasses and sand flowers.

At the table, Walt rolled up his now damp pant legs. He nibbled on some grapes. Geri slapped peanut butter on bread and handed him a sandwich.

He and Geri sat on a jetty made of boulders. Miles started a sand castle near to Geri's feet. He ran into the surf to fill his bucket with drippy sand and brought it back to his creation. And then he'd do it again.

Geri was quiet. She spoke to Walt without making eye contact. Miles paused to listen. Walt was surprised again at how attentive the kid was.

"Henry liked to take photos of birds." Geri looked at the hungry sea gulls that circled around them. "He'd sell them on Shutterstock or to nature magazines for a few extra bucks. One reason he took this job was to be near a couple great bird sanctuaries. He wanted to go to the Aransas National Wildlife Refuge, but he hadn't gone the last time we spoke. It's a large park about three and a half hours south of here. Miles and I will go there and afterwards drive the coast north to about Port Arthur. We will stop at parks and overlooks to see if we can find Henry or Henry's car."

Walt thought it over and didn't give her a hard time. He nodded. "Let me know what your find."

Walt finished his sandwich and watched the surf in silence for a bit. "Time for me to go," he said.

He got up, brushed his backside and waved to Miles.

Geri looked at her son. "Hey Sweetie, want to go look at birds like Daddy does?"

Miles knocked down his castle and waded into the surf to clean out his bucket.

They stopped at a water faucet near the steps to the sea wall to better rinse away the sand on their feet.

At Geri's car, she pulled some wet wipes from her glove box that she used to remove the tar from Miles' feet and then Miles changed into dry clothes.

Walt got into his car, waved and left them to their travels.

Chapter 25 – *Geri* - March 2003

Geri pulled into the wildlife preserve. She slowed and let Miles watch an armadillo cross their path. While Miles' attention was on the wildlife, Geri looked at all the cars in the lot. She shook her head—none of them was Henry's.

After they got out of the car, Geri stroked Miles hair and gave him a hug for as long as the boy would allow. Miles was her light. Without him, Geri tended to sink into darkness, especially when Henry was gone. Geri suspected that Miles knew this – that he understood that it was part of his job to prop her up and bathe her in sunlight. She hated that.

Geri and Miles walked a long boardwalk that looked out at tall grass and water. White whooping cranes with black-tipped wings flew overhead.

"There's an alligator," Miles shrieked. He grabbed his mom's legs and whimpered, "Did an alligator eat daddy?"

"No sweetie, that didn't happen." Geri looked like she wasn't certain.

Miles turned and smiled at her, "Silly alligator. Stay away!" he commanded.

Chapter 26 – *Walt* - March 2003

Walt had two missing persons. To solve this, he had no witnesses, no suspects, no forensic evidence and no autopsy reports. Texas had a huge missing persons problem, meaning more unsolved cases than just about any other state. Given that this case potentially covered at least two jurisdictions, chances of solving it were small. He sent his missing person report to local police in Texas City, Houston and any other jurisdiction where Lynton or Boskova may turn up.

He did have questions. Did these two men have any connection beyond sharing a trailer? Why was one car missing and one left behind? What might have been going on at that oil refinery? Why didn't management report two missing men? Something was amiss.

Walt entered the information he had into CODIS, the federal criminal justice database that matched unknown DNA with offenders, and then he spent some time on his computer reading about the oil refinery business and the Origin Refinery in particular.

Crude oil is a mixture of fluids, gases and contaminants. The mix is determined by where it's pulled out of the ground. If not immediately needed, it's stored in salt caves in atmospheric pressure containers. At refineries impurities are taken out and additives are mixed in with the oil to prolong shelf life and make it more stable—just like the refinery worker said. This was interesting. Over time these additives degrade. *Crude is refined at places like Origin to produce gas, heating oil, diesel, jet fuel, tar, asphalt, paraffin, and nylons.* Walt wanted a copy of Origins' current annual report to see where they made their money. He went to see Tula Guzman, the forensic accountant.

Tula was mid-forties, but she looked mid-thirties. Her sleek, black hair hung down to her waist when she didn't have it gathered into a thick braid like she did today.

"Hey," Walt said as he entered her lair. Tula used a lighted magnifying lamp. She was bent over a stack of paper to examine tiny numbers written in gray ink.

"Got room in your schedule for me?"

Tula looked up and smiled, "What you got," she asked. She looked at his nearly empty hands, with the exception of one piece of paper.

"Can you get the annual report and anything else you can think of for Origin Oil Refinery in Texas City. I'm interested in their financial situation." He handed her a copy of the page of names and number that Geri had provided. "What I got is two missing men from there."

Tula started making notes on the back of the top sheet of her stack of papers. She was great at finding the least little thing, even the notes that she wrote and left all over the place. Walt felt better already.

Walt went back to his office. He called the Environmental Protection Agency and asked about the safety record of Origin Refinery.

A young investigator said, "Origin has an abysmal record. We've dinged them a bunch of times about equipment failure and safety infractions."

"Why haven't they been shut down?"

"Because they don't have that many more than other refineries."

"So, what might happen?" Walt asked. "What were they dinged for?"

"Oil refineries are dangerous places to work, prone to explosions and fires."

"I didn't see any evidence of a fire. What else?

"You're working with chemicals. Some are quite toxic

and can release like an acid into the air."

"Say more." Walt was intrigued.

"Hydrogen sulfide is a gas that's routinely generated during all stages of processing. It's insidious. The first thing it impacts is your nose, so you don't know that you're breathing it until it's too late.

"It could kill you?

"Easily."

Chapter 27 – *Walt* -March 2003

Walt's section chief had glared at him. "You think we're made of money?"

Walt had told him that he planned to drive to Tomball, Texas to visit Eitan Boskova's wife. And then, he might go from Tomball, which was about forty miles north of Texas City, to the main offices of Origin in Houston.

"What does gas cost now— a dollar?" his boss complained. "I'm not even sure this is your case. Give it to Texas City."

"We don't know where Henry Lynton was when he disappeared. Austin is his home. He was expected here. He was reported missing from here."

"Then why do you keep looking there?"

Finally, his boss had relented on him going to Tomball, but said no way on his side trip to Houston.

"You've got a phone, right?" his boss said to punctuate the point.

Walt thought that was probably alright.

He was strangely drawn to this case and didn't mind making the two and half hour drive from Austin to Tomball. It gave him time to think.

Helena Boskova lived in a small, yellow house in a neighborhood of similar small, neat houses. Inside, the furniture was nice, but not new. The paintings on the walls were prints of old masters. Begonias in clay pots lined the window sill. She stacked books by British romance authors on the coffee table.

Helena brought out two Cokes in glasses with ice and

packaged cookies neatly placed on a serving dish. She set two paper napkins decorated with flowers and birds by the drinks.

Walt guessed that she was a good decade younger than her husband, somewhere around twenty years old. She had bouncy brown hair and a plump little body.

"You really think he's missing?" she asked.

"I do," Walt said. "What was he like, your husband?" Walt startled at his use of the past tense. He shouldn't have done that even if he believed it to be true, but Helena didn't seem to notice.

Helena was silent for a minute. "He's a plodder. He slogs through each day happy to provide for us. He wants the oil refinery job to turn into something permanent. If it does, we're going to get a little house on the beach in Kemah or Galveston." She paused, looked at Walt. "I guess I'm not moving to the beach, huh?"

I guess she did notice the past tense. "He's missing. That's all we know." He changed the subject. "How did you two meet?" Walt asked.

"Foster care. He was my big brother for almost a year. He took care of me. He's been taking care of me ever since."

"Does he like his job at the refinery? Is there anything or anyone he complained about?"

"Not so's I noticed."

Walt wondered if she would notice at all. "Do you work?" he asked.

"I've been looking for just the right thing. I need to set my career path in the best direction."

"How do you and Eitan get along?

"Everything's good with us."

Sure. Everything was okeydokey. "He doesn't mind you waiting to find that perfect job. He doesn't want you to get something, anything that will help out?"

"How'd you know? You sound just like him."

Walt was still for a minute to see what would come out.

"He loves me," Helena said.

Walt bet he did. He bet that his was all the love in their relationship. He ate a cookie and stood up to leave. "Did you ever meet his night manager? Guy named Alonzo or Lonny Rossi?"

"No. I've never been there. Nobody's ever comes here."

"Thanks," he said.

That's who Walt really wanted to talk to, but he hadn't been able to find a trace of him. At least Walt knew he was alive after that Thursday night.

Another forty minutes of driving and he'd be at the refinery. He could talk to the night crew. Walt decided to ignore his chief's worry about the high price of gas.

Chapter 28 – *Walt* - March 2003

As he approached Texas City, Walt saw fire and black smoke spurting from three tall towers. He remembered what he'd read about flares. Crude oil with a high sulfur content is called "sour." It can emit hydrogen sulfide or H2S at any point in processing, including during storage. At low concentrations, it smells like rotten eggs. At high concentrations, its heavier than air and travels along the ground. H2S deadens the sense of smell and can impact your breathing before you know it. Monitoring equipment is used to test the air for H2S gas. If there is too much, it is routinely "flared." Fluids are separated from the gases. Gases are vented into the atmosphere and burnt off. Walt assumed this is what he was seeing.

It was midnight, a couple hours until the night shift ended. There were only a few numbers on the phone bills that Geri provided that were from Texas City. One was a combination sports bar and German pub called The Wurst Bar. The bar was near the refinery, served food and drink, so Walt guessed that this was a place that he hung out with his co-workers.

Walt walked into the smell of stale beer and sauerkraut. It was dark, loud and crowded. Still, Walt didn't have a problem locating a table of oil refinery workers. Most had burgers and beers in front of them, watching while a couple others threw darts. Walt observed for a few minutes, but didn't see anything amiss. He bought a pitcher of beer and approached. He set the beer on the table.

"Can I get in on this?" Walt asked meaning the dart game.

"Dollar a point," a brash guy in an Origin gimmie cap said.

Walt nodded and the brazen guy picked up his darts. They played a few turns. Walt examined the score board showing high scores. "Hope you aren't this EB guy," Walt said. "High scorer."

"Elvis. Elvis Brown," he said and held out a hand.

"How you doin', Elvis? Walt Liskin." Ed slammed back a beer, so Walt took a few sips. "I was thinking EB could be Eitan Boskova — the missing man."

"Who are you?"

Walt pulled out his badge. "I'm looking for Henry Lynton and Eitan Boskova. You know them?"

The men just stared at him.

"They're missing. That's all I'm looking for."

"Don't know them, but might have heard something about that," Elvis said.

"Heard what?"

"A lot of stuff has been going missing from the refinery, you know, Origin."

"What kind of stuff?"

"Don't know. Refinery stuff. Vehicles, equipment, barrels."

"Money?"

Elvis shrugged.

Walt hung out a while longer, but these men didn't know anything.

People were coming and going when he arrived at the refinery. It was shift change. He sat on the hood of his car and watched. Many of the men exiting wore respirators and heavy gloves.

As he walked out, one guy tried to talk to one man

who ignored him and then another who also ignored him. A talker, Walt thought. "Hey," he said and nodded for the man to come over.

The man approached warily.

"Accident today?" Walt asked, but even a talker knew better than to answer that. "I'm looking for Lonny Rossi. You know him?"

"Gone. Just up and left. Nobody knows why."

"I heard he quit."

"You a reporter?"

"No."

"Heard that too. Something hinky with that. That's for sure."

"Why so?"

"Sure you're not a reporter?"

Walt discretely held out his badge.

"The cough. He had the red eyes and the cough. I think there was an accident with the H2S. That's what I think."

As the guy walked to his car, Walt noticed another man, a skinny guy, who had pulled his car into the slot next to where Walt parked his vehicle. The second guy leaned against the hood exactly as Walt had been doing a few minutes ago. Walt kept the man in sight, but didn't look directly at him.

Walt kept his distance. He pulled out his cell phone and called a rookie. "Get your partner. You two start calling every hospital in say one hundred miles of Texas City."

"But that includes all of Houston."

"Yeah, it does. You're looking for anyone who has symptoms of exposure to toxic gas."

The skinny guy ambled over to him. He held up a plastic placard that identified him as a reporter for *The Houston Chronicle*.

"What can you tell me about the accident and cover up a couple weeks ago?" the reporter asked.

"Were you here on that day?"

"No, but I came out the next day."

"What makes you think there was an accident?"

"I saw big bosses hanging out and a clean-up crew in hazmat suites with my own two peepers," the reporter replied. "Your turn."

Why not, thought Walt. "Two men, temporary contractors, went missing that night. I'm looking for them."

"I can help with that."

"I'll see about names and pictures," Walt said. "Who's the supervisor working now? You know?"

"Names Elvis Brown. Good luck getting anything out of him. That's him coming in now, half hour late wouldn't you know."

Walt saw a tough-looking man in a nice suit and tie walking across the parking lot. A company man, he thought, a roughneck at one time, but no longer. Definitely not the same man as in the bar. Yeah, the Elvis from the bar walked toward the entrance behind real Elvis and flipped him when Elvis got close. "May I have a word?"

"What can I do for you?" Elvis had a bit of a West Texas twang. He'd moved up instead of being moved in. Maybe that meant he cared about the lives of his men. Walt stole the approach of the reporter.

"I was wondering what you could tell me about the accident on May 21."

"I wasn't working in May. I started this job on June 1."

"You're the night manager, right?"

He nodded.

"You must know something about what's going on."

"Anything I would have to say would be hearsay."

Walt noted the legal term. Not rumors or speculation—hearsay.

Elvis stared at the reporter who was lurking near them.

Walt gave the reporter a jerk of his head to indicate that he should back off. The reporter strolled back to his car.

"Anything I say is off the record," Elvis said. "You can't turn around and tell him."

"Sure."

"We don't know what happened to those men. I swear we don't. But I heard that that same night a bunch of barrels of oil were stolen and I'd say it's not the first time."

"How many barrels?"

"At least six."

"Did you report it?"

"This plant is one inch from being shut down for safety violations. That's my guess why they would rather cover it up."

"I'd like to get a copy of your annual report," Walt asked. "Any other information you can share."

"It will have to come from the main office. I'll have my secretary take care of it."

"Thanks." Walt handed Elvis a business card. "What do you think happened to those men?"

"I think they got caught."

"How far might a cover up go?"

"Your guess is as good as mine."

Part III

Chapter 29 – *Walt* - Monday, March 30, 2026

Walt was in his office when six-year-old Maddox Roget and his mother, Juliette, appeared. They walked the path to his desk. Walt had a moment of déjà vu that reminded him of Geri and Miles' first appearance twenty years ago. Like Geri, this woman was petit and overwhelmed by a shoulder bag, but unlike Geri's long, fair hair, his woman's hair was curly, short and brown. Maddox, small and frail for his age, was clutching something in his left hand.

Juliette and Maddox told him about a volleyball party they had attended over the weekend. "Maddox wanted to go on the rope swing at the river with the older boys," Juliette explained.

"The big boys jump from the giant rock," Maddox said, "and swing out over the river making a big splash when they fall."

"You're too small for the rope swing," his mother said, "and you don't swim well enough yet."

"But Nat was there."

"His older brother, Nathan," his mom filled in. "He's thirteen. Nathan picks him up into his arms…"

Walt put his finger to his lips so Mom wouldn't take over.

"Nat said to hold tight. I held my breath and we jumped. The water went over my head and up my nose. It was scary." Maddox laughed. "I wanted to do it again, but Mom told me to go play in the lagoon with the little kids."

She gave him that look that said you're a little kid.

Walt suspected that Maddox just wanted to be a boy like his brother, but Mom wasn't ready to let him.

"Did you play in the lagoon?" Walt asked.

Maddox nodded. "I kicked up the water with a stick, but the water was stinky. I looked at some green swamp plants and then I got some rocks, but I didn't wash them there in the smelly water. I went to the river's edge. Have you ever seen how water brings out their colors?"

"I have seen that," Walt said. "What happened next?"

"There were some old animal bones with the rocks."

"Cool." Walt could picture Maddox turning the bones over and over in his hands, wondering what animal they were from.

"I showed them to my friend, but he wanted them, so I put the bones into my pocket."

"To figure out later what kind of bones they were?"

Maddox nodded. "I thought Nathan would help me. He's good at figuring things out."

"Is that them?" Walt pointed to the plastic sandwich bag in Maddox' hand. He handed them over. "Thank you," Walt said. "You told that really well." Walt handed Maddox a couple of dollars. "You know how to get yourself a soda out of the machine?" he asked.

Maddox nodded and glanced at his mother who sported a grimace, but agreed that he could have one.

"Mira?" Walt asked after Maddox left.

"Mira Ashe. It was her party. She owns the land." Juliette pointed to the bone. "I found it on his dresser. I'm a nurse. I knew right away what it was." A phalange. Left index finger.

Walt wanted to instantly send a forensic team to the lagoon to search, but it was private land. He'd go see if he could get permission to have a look around.

"I went back a couple days later while Maddox was in

school," his mom said as she rummaged around in her big bag, "but all I found was this old cap."

Walt nearly choked. It was old, tattered, dirty and from Origin Oil Refinery.

Almost twenty years and there had been no sign of Henry Lynton. He was completely gone, as was Eitan Boskova whose wife didn't care. Mrs. Boskova had her husband declared dead so she could remarry. Walt had asked her about it.

"If he's left me, I don't want him back and if he's dead there is nothing I can do about that. Life goes on," she had told Walt.

But Geri Lynton needed 'closure.' She needed to know what had happened to her husband. She needed to understand.

And Miles, Geri's observant, little son who would make a good investigator, was still working the case — nearly twenty years later.

Chapter 30 – *Walt* – Monday, March 30, 2026

As soon as Maddox and his mom left Walt's office, he walked to the crime lab. He handed them the old ball cap and the piece of fingerbone.

"Could you put a rush on it?" Walt asked. "I know some people that have been waiting a long time for an answer."

The lab guy looked sympathetic. "I can't do that. It wouldn't stand up next to something fresh, but I'll give it as much priority as I can."

Walt pulled out his old case files for the hundredth time and gave them another hard read, hoping something would jump out at him after all this time. Nothing did.

What Walt wanted was warrants to search and dig at that lagoon, but the section chief said that he needed more evidence. The chief, his boss, said that that finger could have floated there from anywhere, and the cap wasn't enough on its on to tie it to the missing men. He had to wait for the DNA results before he could go forward. Walt wrote up the paperwork and had it ready to go.

And so, he waited.

He took a little drive by the land, but no one was around to give him permission to search. Still, he took a little walk. He found nothing more on the surface by the lagoon.

He waited two weeks.

Walt's section chief drifted by his office door. "What're you working on?" he asked.

Likely the chief had noticed that he wasn't spending as much time as the chief thought he should on current cases.

"I got a cold case that's stuck with me hard."

The chief gave him a look that begged for an explanation. "What is it?"

"Two men that disappeared off the face of the earth twenty years ago. I've been working it intermittently since. It's still assigned to me."

"That fingerbone related?"

Walt nodded.

"I understand about cases that make you crazy, but we have plenty enough of crazy as it is without looking into the past. That finger waited twenty years. Nobody is going anywhere."

"I think I can come up with something. New methods. New technology."

"Who you going after?"

"Not sure yet?"

"Okay. No resources. No slacking on current cases. And no pissing anyone off."

"Yes, sir. Polite all the way."

"You got one week to come up with something to intrigue me or its back to the cold case file."

His chief had put a window on it, but refused to give him help so that he could meet it. The chief liked deadlines and gave them out even when it made no sense. Thankfully, if something came up, especially something concrete like DNA, Walt knew he could be convinced to extend.

Walt sat at his desk and stared at a picture on his wall. Kid art. Walt could think of a good resource that would be happy to help and wouldn't cost the chief a thing. He thought long and hard before he made that call.

"Hey Walt. Good to hear from you," Miles, now twenty-seven years old, said when he picked up the call.

"Got some stinky water here. It's about forty miles

upstream from Austin. Nasty." Walt started slow.

"Yeah?"

"You think you could get assigned here for a couple months?" Miles was now an investigator for the Environmental Protection Agency out of Washington D.C.

"I can check it out. When do you need me?"

"How's tomorrow work for you?"

Miles was silent for a minute. "What's up, Walt?" he asked.

"I don't know anything yet. Don't get your hopes up," Walt said even though his hopes were high. "I may or may not have new evidence."

"I'll be there in the morning. See you soon."

Chapter 31 – *Miles* – Thursday, April 2, 2026

Miles pulled into the Austin Police Department garage. He parked in a visitor spot, got out of his car and strolled into the station. At reception, he signed in and got a visitor badge. He went to the elevator and hit three.

He walked across the common area where the officers sat spaced a few feet apart from each other to a man with salt and pepper hair who sat at a desk crammed into a too small office space.

"Hey Walt," Miles said as he crammed himself into a visitor's chair. "So, is this office an upgrade from your desk out there?" He pointed to the common area. Walt stretched out, highlighting to Miles that all the legroom was on his side of the desk.

Miles noticed a child's drawing framed on the wall behind the desk. It was a birthday card Miles had made for Walt when he was nine. It was intended to remind Walt to keep up the search. Apparently, it had worked. Miles had had brief contact with Walt every year up until now.

"How do you want to approach this?" he asked Walt.

"We need to get on that land, but I can't get a warrant without more. That might take another week, maybe two." Walt smiled at him as he handed over a driver's license photo. "The owner is a pretty young woman who has a volleyball party every weekend."

"I haven't played much volleyball," Miles said.

Walt handed him a rule book for the game. "Time to learn."

Chapter 32 – *Miles* - Thursday, April 30, 2026

Miles followed the same path back to Walt's office that he had taken several week before. In that time, he had made contact with Mira and managed a superficial search of the land as well as conducted casual interviews over the weekend. Mira had been welcoming and generous. She had an easy smile and an easy manner. He liked her much more than he imagined possible. He wanted to touch her, not investigate her.

Miles had come clean and introduced Mira to Walt after his softball game last night. He wished he had been more straight with her from the start. It would matter if she thought he was a liar. She listened quietly and intently to everything he had to say. She was warm and polite as he drove her back to her car at the ball field. He had no clue how she had taken all he had said.

"Got anything?" Miles asked Walt.

"I checked out the volleyball names you sent to me. Not much on any of them. Parking tickets here and there. Jimmie Rey Yazzie was a runaway, fled when he was fifteen, but no one seems to be looking for him. His father's a migrant worker—follows the pecans. His mother teaches native American children. Jimmie Rey's also got a couple of DUI's in Arizona."

Miles pulled some papers from his pack. "None of the volleyballers pop for me. They take good care of the land, clean-up after themselves, recycle and compost. Mira, in particular, was really upset by the pollution in the lagoon."

"Plus, they're all too young. Was there anyone there

who was old enough to be your father?"

"No."

"So, we still have no suspects?"

"I haven't ruled anyone out, but, yeah, no good ones." Miles handed the papers to Walt.

Walt looked at the report in his hands. "You've already gotten the results on the water testing."

"No. Mira was doing her own investigation. She had the water and the soil tested, but just in the area around that polluted lagoon. Check it out."

"Interesting," Walt said. "Who is Mira investigating?"

"Young men with blond hair. A store owner nearby told her she had seen a young guy with fair hair on her property when he shouldn't be."

"So, you?" Walt ruffled his blond locks.

"Yeah. Plus, she has two others: Jayson Brookshire and Riley Miller."

"Why this Miller guy?"

"I'm not sure."

"And Brookshire?"

"That's something to check into. That's what I'm going to do next. Talk to him," Miles said. He and Mira had decided that, as a trained investigator, it would be best if he approached Jayson Brookshire about his intentions for the land and his interest in Mira.

Chapter 33 – *Jayson* - Thursday, April 30, 2026

Jayson's office had plush area rugs over dark wood floors and Swedish furniture, but it didn't please him. He stood looking out his third story window, not really seeing his view of the Colorado River, called Lady Bird Lake as it ran through downtown Austin. He hummed softly under his breath, tapping his fingers on the window pane. It was a cloudless day outside. Bright sunshine was muted by the tinted glass.

His phone rang.

"Yes."

"There's a gentleman to see you."

"I'm not expecting anyone." Jayson could hear talking in the background.

"He says to tell you it's Miles Lynton from last Saturday."

"Oh. Okay. Send him in." He stood and adjusted the collar of his navy suit jacket.

Miles reached out and took Jayson's hand when he offered it.

"How's Jimmy Rey?" Jayson asked.

"Back in the hospital, I'm afraid. He picked up a flu bug. Probably got it at the hospital in the first place. Hospital was crowded with folks with it."

Jayson pointed to a chair and Miles sat in it. Jayson took his measure. "Jimmy Rey," he said. "He's got an interesting look. Where's he from?" Jayson asked. "You know?"

Miles sounded like he was giving a report. "His

mother was a Navaho from the Four Corners area. She went missing when he was fourteen and they found her a year later teaching kids on the reservation." Jayson wondered if she was hiding out, likely from an abusive husband—a man she had left her son with. Miles confirmed this with his next comment. "His father is half-Mexican from Juarez and half white. Jimmy Rey grew up on the road in New Mexico and Arizona, but mostly, he lived in Phoenix. Apparently he and his Dad didn't get along so well as Jimmy Rey walked away at age fifteen and no one ever reported it."

"Phoenix?"

"You know. It's a dry heat. It gets hot, up to about one hundred and thirty at the worst. Dust floats in the air like a cloud. The ground is barren dirt unless you flood it regularly with water. There is little rainfall except in late summer when the wind brings in the sand and rain pounds it into everything. You know, it's a desert."

"Sounds like you don't think much of the desert," Jayson said.

"No. I love it. Went to the Grand Canyon with my parents when I was little. I've hiked and rafted there several times since then."

"Is that why you became an EPA investigator?" Jayson had done his own research.

"Partly," Miles said.

"I admire what you do. It's important." Jayson said. "We have to learn to live within our natural resources: air, water, soil."

"Absolutely."

"I read the world can only support two billion people with the resources we have. We have six billion and that will double in the next four decades. Is that true?"

"I haven't heard that statistic," Miles said, "but it

doesn't sound wrong."

"Is it too late for humans?"

"We're definitely on the downhill slide," Miles said, "past the tipping point. We have to do all we can, otherwise we don't deserve this planet. That's another part of why I'm with the EPA."

Jayson let the topic go. "What can I do for you today?" he asked.

"Mira wishes you to know that she does not want to see herself or any of her friends come to harm. She will avoid that at any cost."

Jayson was stunned into silence.

Miles also sat in silence.

Jayson thought it felt like a game. Who would break first? Well, it wouldn't be him. He'd miss every appointment for the rest of the day if need be. Jayson thought about what Miles said - she will avoid harm at any cost. He looked out the window without seeing. Harm.

"I like her," Jayson said without thinking about the fact that he was breaking the silence. He turned in time to see the surprise and concern on Miles' face before he covered it.

"Did you know that last Monday someone tried to run her off the road?" Miles said.

Jayson made no attempt to hide his shock. "What!? Is she all right?"

"For now."

"You think that nothing like this happened before I made the offer for her land. You think I must be involved."

"I have to wonder." Miles started the silence game again. He had a good poker face.

"It's my job to obtain the land for my company. I wouldn't hurt her to get it."

"If she were to sell the land to you, do you think the

danger would stop?"

Jayson considered it. "I'm not the owner or decision-maker on this land deal. Within Andover & Associates, I'm a glorified buyer. I don't know what others might do. Andover the third is desperate for this deal to work." *Too desperate,* Jayson thought.

Miles waited for him to say more, but Jayson let him wait. "You think your bosses are capable of violence to get what they want?"

Jayson laughed. "This isn't a thriller novel, but stakes are very high for the company. This isn't all that's on the line."

"What's that mean?"

Jayson stood by the window again. He liked the security of money. He liked his condo, his BMW and his fine suits. He should shut his mouth.

Miles stood. "Thanks for your time."

"Andover isn't the only party to the deal," he said. "I've been buying up land for a consortium. I don't know who else is involved, but they aren't alone."

Miles nodded his thanks before he walked out.

Chapter 34 – *Tula* **- Thursday, April 30, 2026**

Tula Guzman had retired from the Austin Police Department three years ago.

She was one of those people who had no box for her race on census forms, job applications and surveys. She was equal parts Black, White, Native American and Latina. It was only recently that "other" categories began to appear. Before that, she would mark all that applied or nothing at all.

After she retired, Tula took one of those ancestry spit tests and located four distinct locations in the world that made up her history. Tula decided to visit each of those places.

She started at the home of the Jena Band of Choctaw in Grant Parish, Louisiana. Next, she went to Memphis, Tennessee and followed the Trail of Tears to Tahlequah, Oklahoma. Of course, she took a car in lieu of walking. She wasn't being removed by the government from her home, so it went much easier for her. In the end, she spent a few days at the casino in Durant. She won back about half the cost of her trip.

Tula left for home days sooner than she had planned because she got a call from Walt Liskin about the possible reopening of the Henry Lynton/Eitan Boskova case. In a message, he said something about new evidence. Tula had worked as a forensic accountant on that case. At the time, she knew something was off, but she couldn't put her finger on it. That case had haunted her just like it did him.

She called Walt. "New evidence?" she asked.

"Yes. Come see," Walt replied.

"Will you be able to solve it now?" she asked.

"Likely," said Walt.

"I want in."

"The chief will only approve you as a paid consultant if we find something," Walt said.

"I want in," Tula repeated.

"Happy to have your help."

When she arrived, Walt covered Tula in paper, flash drives, and computers. She'd added to this by printing any public financial information she could find on any name that appeared in her documentation. She requested banking records, invoices and inventories and got a surprising amount of data. Mira supplied a box full of her family's private information. Jayson obtained what he could from Andover and Associates. People's idea of privacy had changed a lot in recent years. She spent most of a week going through them all.

Walt had obtained private Origin financial records five years before. Tula wondered why he hadn't called her in then to review them. A thought struck Tula. Maybe he didn't have a warrant. Maybe he got the records some other way and that's why he didn't want to involve her.

Walt stepped into the conference room, her make-shift office for the project. The table was covered with neat stacks of papers, each sporting a post-it note in one of three colors. A map was taped to the wall with circles connected to triangles with lines.

"You've been working," Walt said. "You got something?"

"Maybe. Maybe something."

Walt waited for her to say more.

Tula placed her right palm on a stack of papers. "This accounts for normal business at Origin Refinery." She put her left hand on another stack. "It's backed up by inventory." She pointed. "That stack is something else. It's money that can't be traced back to normal operations. Lots of money. It shows significant missing inventory."

Walt glanced through the summary page she had prepared for each stack.

"This stack is bank records that I was able to trace back to a large, global consortia called Darwin. There were a few side roads, but yes, they paid a lot of money for something."

Walt gave her a blank look.

"They're smugglers," Tula explained.

"Smugglers?" Walt stared at her, not in disbelief, but in something more like relief.

"They pick up something by boat. I think it originates in Mexico City, but I can't prove that. Somehow, likely truck, it goes to Tampico which is a port town." She moved to the map and pointed to an orange circle.

Walt walked over to take a look.

"A boat takes the stuff to an oil derrick in the Gulf of Mexico."

Walt followed her narration with a finger.

"There it's loaded onto a larger ship with regular oil shipments. The ship comes to Origin Oil Refinery."

"Where some guys load it onto a truck and take it where?" Walt said.

"I can't do everything," Tula said.

Chapter 35 – *Walt* - Thursday, April 30, 2026

Miles and Walt sat in a bar waiting for the DNA results to ping on Walt's phone. They wanted to drink, but didn't want to drink too much in case the results were as expected. They were each on their second beer when the ping sounded.

Walt paused for dramatic effect before he opened his email and its attachments. He could get into the detail later, but, for now, he headed straight to the summary.

"What's it say?" Miles looked like the intense little boy Walt remembered.

"They weren't able to get DNA on both," he said. "The cap was inconclusive."

"Well?" Miles pushed.

"The finger belongs to Eitan Boskova."

Miles took a deep breath and let out all the air in his lungs. "The other guy. Enough for a search warrant?"

"Yeah." Walt felt the clicking of a case nearly solved, but he did not feel the satisfaction that usually went along with that. Instead, he felt the finality of Miles' loss. "You okay?" he asked.

"Just get on with it." Miles was tense and shaky.

"I'm asking for both sides of the river as well as the lagoon."

Walt and Miles went back to the office. Walt plugged in some holes on the warrant he had pre-prepared and added a couple photos and the DNA report as attachments.

"I can email it over to the judge," he said.

"Can I walk it? Would that go faster?" Miles was anxious and needed something to do.

"Okay," Walt responded.

While Miles literally fast-walked the warrant, Walt went to see his chief. "Working on a warrant as we speak," he said. "Can I get CSI and some diggers?" Walt asked.

"Two days," his chief said. "Ten people and two days. That's what you get for a twenty-year-old case. Make the best of it."

Walt had a new deadline.

Chapter 36 – *Miles* - Friday, May 1, 2026

Geri Lynton was forty-five, but looked older. Stress had creased around her eyes and under her skin. She hadn't bothered with her hair. It hung loose and lank.

"What do you think they're doing now?" Mom asked Miles. They sat side by side on the living room sofa.

"They're going to start at the lagoon and mark off grids. They've brought dogs and heavy-duty ground penetrating radar. They'll check each grid." It was Thursday morning. Walt had access to resources through Friday end-of-day and Miles thought that worked out fine for Mira. She wouldn't have to cancel the weekend party.

"But he's there?" Mom asked Miles again, but fell silent when no answer came. She had already asked a half dozen times and knew he didn't know the answer.

Miles glanced toward a display of Dad's photos on the wall. He remembered his dad sitting quietly on a rock by the side of a stream with a camera to his eye.

Mom watched him and then made his internal thoughts into words. "Every Saturday, Henry drove to some remote place, hiked into the back country and took beautiful pictures. As soon as you could walk, you wanted to go with your dad. Henry taught you to be still and observe nature. He taught you about the color and life in the natural world."

"They really are beautiful," Miles said about the photos.

"Henry sent ten of his best bird shots to the Audubon Photography Competition. He didn't win the competition, but Audubon did buy one of his photos for the magazine.

Over the next couple of years, they purchased four more. Texas Parks and Wildlife magazine also bought a half dozen of his photos. It wasn't a living yet, but, if he hadn't disappeared, it would have become one." Miles had heard all this many times before.

Miles loved nature too, but he didn't have the eye for photography. And he was scared with what he was seeing in nature these days: floods, fires and scorched earth. Humans were killing their home, and so Miles joined the Environmental Protection Agency as an investigator. He wanted to help to save the natural world both he and his dad loved.

Miles and Walt had stayed friends of a sort since Walt first began to investigate his dad's case. Walt never gave up on finding his father. Walt ran out of avenues to pursue, but he kept in touch with Miles over the years. Both continued to investigate without much success until Maddox Roget showed up in Walt's office with a finger bone.

Even though Miles wasn't a cop, he could have gone to the land to search with Walt's team. He felt certain that Walt would have passed him in, but Miles wanted to wait with Mom. He took her hand.

Miles had found her at eleven o'clock that morning. She had been at work, but he convinced her to take the afternoon off. That's when he told her about the fingerbone and the grid search at the lagoon.

"It may take some time until we're sure one way or another. I don't' want you to get your hopes up." If they found nothing in the official search, Miles doubted that he or Walt would give up.

"But he's there, right?" Mom asked again.

Chapter 37 – *Mira* - Saturday, May 2, 2026

At the Firebrand River, the sky was a collision of black and white. Dark storm clouds in the distance approached in rolling waves across a pale horizon. The air was hot and humid in a way that reminded Mira of baking bread and it held the scent of rain. She just hoped that it rained this time and was not that dry rumbling that streaked the sky. They needed rain so badly.

Mira watched Miles. He had been sitting perfectly still for two hours on the top of the hill that overlooked the tidal pool. In the first two days of the search, they had found nothing on Mira's land. Walt had pled permission for an extra half day out of the chief. They were focusing on the land on the opposite side of the river.

It was almost noon on Saturday, so a few people began to trickle into the field to play volleyball. Mira thought they should be more curious about the goings on, but they weren't. Nothing stopped the game.

Mira strolled up the hill looking for a sign from Miles that it was okay to join him. He smiled. She sat down on the ground close beside him.

"Is there anything we can do for the lagoon water?" she asked.

"I've been thinking about that," Miles answered. "There's a process of pumping pressurized oxygen into the water that sometimes works. The lagoon has a natural separation from the river, so there should be some way to block it off and clean it up."

"Will that protect the river?"

"I have no idea," Miles said. He was not a scientist; he

was an investigator. "There's a few guys I can ask at the EPA."

"I could check with that guy I met at the lab."

"Good idea."

Walt's team had overturned a good part of the river's edge on the opposite shore. The wildflowers were dying in the bright sun on top of the turned ground. It looked like the graveyard that it likely was.

Late yesterday, the techs using the ground-penetrating radar discovered a metal barrel deep within the side of a tall hill. They started digging out the whole hill early this morning. There were high levels of sour crude in the water, so every digger was in full bio-hazard gear to protect from H2S. It was spooky–men in hazmat suits turning over brackish, green dirt. After a couple hours, a rusted, leaking barrel of toxic goo was found, trapped in a container made for the purpose and carted off.

Soon, parts of two near totally decomposed bodies were discovered. Their identity had to be confirmed, but Miles knew without doubt that the bodies were the two missing men. He averted his eyes. He didn't want this image to be what he remembered of his father.

"Will you tell me about your dad's death?" Miles asked Mira.

"My dad?"

"Yes."

"It was horrible," Mira reflected. "One day at work, Dad developed a fever that went up to 104 degrees.

"Where did he work?" Miles asked.

"He did intermittent contract work." She didn't want to tell Miles that he hardly worked at all and when he did, she didn't know what he did. Mira rushed on.

"Did he ever do contract work at Origin Oil Refinery?"

"I don't know."

"What happened next?"

"So, Mom called an ambulance that took him to the hospital. I stayed home that first night with a neighbor, but even when I saw him the next day, he was sick to his stomach, his eyes wouldn't quit tearing and he had a racking cough. The doctors didn't know exactly what was going on, but when they tried to ask him what he'd been doing, he couldn't say for sure. He said he was exposed to something. He didn't know what. They did lots of tests. They treated him for respiratory distress and sepsis. He was a mess for years after and finally his heart began to fail."

"Was it related to the earlier trauma?"

"They say so. Yes. They say his heart had been compromised. They put him on a transplant list, but he wasn't a good candidate. He didn't get a new heart."

"Do you know the date that your father got sick?"

"Not sure. Sometime in the spring of 2003."

"Did they do an autopsy on your dad?" Miles asked.

"I have no idea." Mira looked at him. "That's a weird question."

"How old were you then?" Miles asked.

"Four when he had the accident and twenty-one when he died."

"And he gave you this land in his will?"

"Yes. It's in the hands of a property manager until I graduate from law school. You might talk to him. He was a friend of Dad's."

"Did your dad say anything about what should be done with the land?"

"Dad asked me not to develop it and I really haven't. It's been a great place to play, but I feel that my life is turning in a new direction. I'm not sure I need it any longer. And then I got an offer to sell."

"Interesting timing," Miles said.

What are you getting at?" Mira asked.

Miles hadn't answered when they saw Walt pull into the parking lot. Miles cautiously ambled over to Walt's car. Mira let him go alone, but Walt's expression told them both what they needed to know.

Chapter 38 – *Riley* - Saturday, May 2, 2026

Riley weaved in and out of traffic, barely conscious of doing so. He drove fast, but he was safe. He spun down the gravel road to the river. Dust and rocks flew up behind him as his classic Mustang plowed down the drive.

There were a couple of cop cars in the parking area, but he didn't see any cops.

He jumped out and pulled off his tee shirt, throwing it into the back seat with one hand while opening a cooler and extracting a six-pack of beer with the other. He walked toward the little cabin with the refrigerator.

There she was. As was so often the case these days, Mira was huddled with Miles. Half a dozen other people stood close by. Close to her. She was like the sun and they were all her planets, in constellation, revolving around her. Ever since he told Mira the truth, he had felt like he had lost her light and her warmth. And he hadn't told her the half of how much he cared for her.

She smiled at him, but it wasn't inviting. He didn't walk over. He put the beer in the fridge and went to play a couple games of volleyball.

"Hey Riley," one of the players called out. "This point will take care of this game, and then you can substitute for me."

Riley joined the next game, playing hard. The few dark clouds burned off and it had to be one hundred and four degrees. What wind came was hot and humid and moved the air very little.

They took a short break to drink water and cool down. Riley mopped sweat from his forehead with a towel. He had finished a beer and popped open another when he saw Jayson join Mira and Miles. Jayson had come from the direction of the river. Riley noticed tents and men tramping around the tidal pool. *What were they up to,* he wondered. Riley held the beer tightly without taking a sip.

"Players," someone called. It was the signal that started the next game. The participants ambled onto the make-shift court.

"Hey, you playing?" someone called to him.

"Yeah. Right there." He took his position under the net.

When Riley finished his last game, Mira and Miles had moved to the cold, empty fire pit and were still talking to Jayson. They seemed chummy. Their heads were close together and their faces showed strain.

Why did Miles or Jayson get to sit in the circle? Riley wondered. She hardly knew them. He wanted to sit next to her. He was here first.

Mira was Riley's contact with the human race. He didn't have many friends beyond her and the people in her life that she shared with him. He would do anything to win back her favor.

A man with salt and pepper hair came out of the trees and walked toward the fire pit. He was followed by two cops in uniform. With their heads lowered, the cops carried out equipment boxes and loaded up a couple of trucks.

Riley walked toward the fire pit.

Chapter 39 – *Miles* - Saturday, May 2, 2026

The volleyball players took a break at about one o'clock for lunch and people gathered around the cold fire pit to think about making food. Miles had decided this would be the best time to talk to the regulars.

"Everyone," Miles said. "Most of you know that I'm Miles Lynton, but what you probably don't know is that I'm an investigator for the Environmental Protection Agency." He showed a badge. He looked into the faces of his new friends to see if he could determine what they thought of this revelation. He couldn't tell. He nodded to Walt. "This is Austin Police Detective Walt Liskin. Walt held up his badge. Walt and I have partnered to work a twenty-year-old case."

"Cool and quite cold. And that brings you here?" Riley asked, he obviously being smarter than for which Miles had given him credit.

"You guys know Maddox Roget. Six-year-old boy," Walt said. Heads nodded all around. Everyone knew Maddox. He was loud and exuberant, but in a charming way.

"We haven't seen him," Riley said as he looked around. "Is he okay?"

"He found a phalange beside the Firebrand River," Walt said.

"A finger bone," Miles clarified.

Walt pointed toward the river where there was a large roped off area barely visible in the trees. "We just finished our search and found the bones of two men."

"I get him," Riley said, pointing at Walt, "but why

does the EPA care?" Riley looked at him with distain. Miles wondered why Riley seemed to dislike him so much.

He took over the conversation again. "You know the lagoon where the little kids like to play. You've seen it go foul and stinky. Mira had the water tested. She was concerned for the health of your children."

Several mothers shot Mira shocked looks.

"I had the kids get out of the water as soon as I saw something was wrong," Mira snapped angrily. "You know that." She got up and stomped to her cabin. She went inside and slammed the door.

Wow, Miles thought. *Mira has a temper.* She was angry and he didn't have a clue as to why, but he worried that she was mad at him.

"This is a potentially serious situation," Walt continued. "Don't go into the marked areas. Don't let your kids go there. Keep an eye on them or we will have to shut down this party and send you all home."

The regulars looked sufficiently wary.

Miles went on. "The green tint and rotting smell are caused by cyanobacteria or more familiarly called toxic blue-green algae.

"That's what's polluting the pond? Algae?" someone whose name he did not know asked.

"Yes. In part. Essentially, the algae consumed all the oxygen from the lagoon killing the plants and fish underneath it. You have a hypoxic dead zone. The lagoon is gone."

"Are my kids in danger?" asked a mother.

"Usually algae isn't harmful to people, but don't take any chances. Your kids can't swim there anymore unless or until we can clean it up."

"What about the river? Will the river be okay?"

"The river may improve over time," Miles said.

"What happened?" asked Riley. "Why did the water go bad?" He looked around at the pristine environment. He held out his hands to make his point.

"You're right," Miles said. "There are no triggers in the immediate area. No farms, no factories, nothing like that, but the lab results showed high amounts of hydrogen sulfides. This usually comes from the oil refining process."

"So, how'd it get here?"

"We have a theory." Miles turned to Walt.

Walt stood and continued. "Almost twenty years ago, two men went missing from a Texas City oil refinery along with what they thought were six barrels of refined oil, but I believe that at least one of those barrels contained the toxic elimination from oil processing. We found the bodies of two men by the river. We believe, but can't yet prove, that someone killed these two men and buried them here along with the toxic barrel. We'll have to wait for analysis to discover what is in the barrel."

Silence all around.

"There are still five barrels missing. Any ideas? Miles asked.

The group looked around at the hills that surrounded them, the trees lush with green leaves, the meadow dotted with wildflowers. It was their place in the world and they loved it.

"Dottie," Riley said.

Nods all round. "Yeah Dottie."

"Dottie?" asked Walt.

"She's been around forever. She runs the little store down the road. If there is anything to know, she knows it."

"Okay. Dottie, then," Miles said.

Everyone stood up.

Miles smiled. "Walt and I will go. You guys go back to your game. Have fun." He turned to Walt. "Let me get

Mira. It might help to have her for an introduction, so Dottie will talk to us."

Walt nodded.

Chapter 40 – *Miles* - Saturday, May 2, 2026

Miles knocked on the door to her cabin, but when Mira didn't answer, he let himself in.

She sat on the bed. The bedclothes were rumpled into a ball around her. She had likely searched for snakes. Mira had her computer in her lap doing searches. Her mouth was set into a grim, unhappy line. She glared at Miles. She had barely said a word to him in hours, instead doing her best to hide away.

"We're going to go ask Dottie some questions. Would you like to come with us?" Miles asked.

Mira picked up her purse and stomped out of the cabin. She got into the back seat of Walt's car, and so he took the front passenger seat. Walt wrinkled his brow to ask a question. Miles shrugged to say he didn't know.

When Mira, Walt and Miles got to the little store, it was closed with no indication of when it might open again.

Mira spoke to Walt. "Sometimes, Dottie will step away for a few minutes, but she always leaves a little clock on the door handle that shows by its hands when she will return. Dottie works at the store and lives above. She is nearly always here."

Miles plopped down on one of the porch chairs to wait, trying to hide that he was overwhelmed by his sense of foreboding.

Mira ran to the nearest neighbor and pounded on the door. Miles followed, but not too close. One of the ancient men, stooped and gnarled, who liked to sit on Dottie's porch answered.

"What's happened?" Mira asked. "Where's Dottie?"

"Didn't you hear?" the old man said. "She picked up the flu and they had to take her to the hospital."

"Is she okay?"

"I don't know." The old man looked unmoored, lost at sea.

"Jimmy Rey and Andee have the flu too," Mira said. This was the first that Miles had heard of it. She had told no one.

The old man looked at her accusingly like her friends brought this disease to Dottie.

"They haven't been to the land since Jimmy Rey was bitten by that snake." Mira answered his glare. "They likely picked up the flu bug in the hospital." She wasn't in a mood to put up with anything. "I'll go to town and find out about Dottie. About all of them." Mira softened her voice a bit. "I'll let you know," she said as she gently held his hand.

Mira went to Walt's car and the three of them drove back to the land in silence. Mira headed for her cabin.

"What's up with her?" Walt asked.

"I don't know, but I'm gonna find out," Miles answered.

"Might be best to leave her alone for a bit."

But Mira left her cabin right away, slamming the door and locking it, with her overnight bag packed. She headed for her car. Before she could get her door open and make her escape, Miles placed a gentle hand on her hand that held her keys.

"What?" Miles asked, poetic with his inquiry.

"I've been thinking a lot about the questions you asked when we were up on the hill. When did he get sick? Where was he? So, does it all line up?" Mira asked.

Miles didn't answer.

"You think my father had something to do with the

death of those two men. That's why you're here. That's why you came. The look on Mira's face was sad, dejected. She spoke in a whisper when she said, "You're in my way."

Chapter 41 – *Mira* - Saturday, May 2, 2026

Tears rolled down Mira's cheeks as she left her property. She hardly noticed the drive toward Andee's house in Austin. She planned to pick up some of Andee's essentials and take them to the hospital, but that was just an excuse. She wanted to be with her friends. The road was blurry, and so she stopped at a roadside rest stop for a few minutes to dry her eyes, blow her nose and calm her breathing.

When she moved on, she felt pleased at the speed at which she was able to travel—let's face it, the speed at which she was able to run away from Miles. Traffic was light. It felt odd to be on a road that was nearly empty.

She turned on the radio. The news was on. She had missed the story's beginning, but it caught her attention.

"The death toll is estimated at twenty-four thousand already," the newscaster said. It sounded like that Rory newscaster guy, Isa's boyfriend. "It is presumed that that number is underestimated and will rise quickly."

Mira turned off the radio. She didn't want to hear about it. She prayed it was another fire, tornado or earthquake, not the new flu. All the news seemed to be any more was a rising death toll.

It wasn't until she parked in front of Andee's apartment complex that she was struck by how very strange the quiet was, especially for a Saturday afternoon. There was a small playscape on the side of the building. Mira rarely saw it empty on weekend days, but it was today.

Mira looked to her left. Two empty spaces down was a car. Andee's mother, Kay, sat behind the wheel, a look of horror on her face. She was ugly crying, slime trailing from her nose.

Mira rushed over and tapped the window startling Kay. Mira held up a box of tissues. In a minute, Kay recognized her and opened the window. She gasped for air and pushed out one word "hospital."

"Jimmy Rey?" Mira asked.

Andee's mom shook her head. "Dead," she struggled to say.

That can't be right, Mira thought. *That can't be true.*

"Yesterday," Kay went on.

"I talked to him on the phone just a couple days ago. He had the flu, just the flu." Mira had been feeling a level of panic since the night she had spent at the hospital, but she wouldn't allow herself to feel it. She couldn't stand another flu outbreak. In her mind, she wouldn't allow it to be true.

"Very contagious, deadly." Kay blew her nose once and then again. "Everywhere," she said still unable to make whole sentences.

Kay slammed Mira with the car door. She leaned her head out of the car and threw up just missing Mira's shoes. She vomited again while Mira rubbed circles on her back. Kay continued with dry heaves for another minute.

Mira sunk to the driver's side running board, sitting on it next to Kay. Mira's head fell on Kay's back. Mira held Kay in her arms as her own tears soaked the back of Kay's shirt.

Mira refused to believe that one of her two best friends had died and she knew nothing about it. What was Kay saying? *This can't be right.*

"Can I call someone for you?" Mira asked.

"No." Kay sat back up and pulled the door shut. Mira had to jump out of the way.

Mira walked to her own car, but didn't get in. Andee's mom liked Jimmy Rey well enough, but Mira couldn't see her having this reaction to the news of his death. It was Andee. Something had happened to Andee.

Mira ran up the steps to Andee's second floor apartment. She opened the door with her own key, and screamed inside calling Andee's name, but no one was there.

When Mira rushed outside to the second-floor railing, she saw Kay's car spin out of the parking lot and onto the street. It was heading east probably toward the hospital. Mira ran to her own car and chased after Kay, but she had too much of a lead and Mira lost her.

The hospital parking lot was full. The overage was parked along the sides of the road as well as anywhere else that could hold a car. Mira walked well over two miles from where she'd left her car until she could even see the doors of the hospital.

Hordes of people, many wearing masks they likely hadn't touched since the declared end of COVID-19, banged on the outside double doors and ranted, but no one was given entry. It looked like a scene from a horror movie. Mira struggled through the crowd, gaining a couple feet every few minutes.

There was a sign on the left door that said, "No visitors" and a sign on the right door that said. "Full" in huge letters with a caption. "We have reached capacity." Below that, it listed the names and addresses of other hospitals and the morgue.

Mira peeked through the glass. The outer doors had a metal grate to cover them, but she could see a bit of the waiting room and hallways. They were packed with sick patients in beds. A nurse in full hazmat suit walked between the sick and dying.

A volunteer in an N95 mask and protective clothes opened the inner door and slipped through; however, she didn't open the outer door. People were yelling at her so you could barely make out what she was saying.

"Get as much food and water as you can and then go home." She yelled through the nighttime emergency speaker. "Lock yourselves inside. Don't let anyone in with your family. Duct tape the cracks around your windows and doors. This flu is extremely infectious."

No one was paying her any attention, including Mira. They yelled and pounded on the glass. Like Mira, all they wanted was to get inside and figure out what happened to their friends and family.

"Go home," the volunteer said again. "Save yourself. There is nothing you can do for anyone inside this building." The woman looked beyond frustrated. "Including me," she yelled.

As Mira watched, she taped up a list on the window. She stared at it. It was labeled, "Today's Dead."

The crowd rushed forward, knocking Mira off her feet. She covered her head with her hands as she was squished against the outside wall. Someone kicked her in the hip. Mira scooted an inch at a time away from the window with the list and the masses anxious to read it.

"Back up. Out of the way." Andee's mom was hitting the crowd around Mira with her purse. She made a little space and pulled Mira to her feet. She and Kay backed away from the list.

"Thanks," Mira said.

"We'll never get close enough," Kay said. "They'll put the list of today's dead online by tonight. Yesterday, it was printed in the paper. That's where I saw Jimmy Rey's name, but now it's only online. The guy who knew how to use the paper cut and fold machine died yesterday. No more newspaper."

"What's going on?" Mira asked.

"It's the end of the world," Kay looked surprised at the question. "They had a special show about it on television last night. It's on YouTube if you want to see it." Kay waved as she walked away. "Thanks for the Kleenex," she called over her shoulder. "Be well!"

Chapter 42 – *Mira* - Saturday, May 2, 2026

Mira sat on the curb at the far end of the parking lot. Going home with no answers was not in Mira's plan. She hadn't told anyone this, but she was not with her father when he died. She was at a party having fun. Her father died alone. She wondered if he had felt unloved.

She debated the sheer craziness of going into the hospital against the turmoil of leaving her friends, whom she loved more than herself, on their own. She hadn't gotten sick that night when Jimmy Rey and Andee both had. Maybe she had a natural immunity. *Or she was really lucky,* she thought.

Mira thought about that volunteer in the glass door. The nurse thought she would not survive, but she was there anyway. Even if Mira didn't survive it, people in that hospital needed help. They needed love. They needed someone to be there at the end so they would not die alone.

She was getting into that hospital. She walked the perimeter, checking every door she came upon. All locked. She stepped back about twenty feet. The windows appeared to be the kind that did not open. None on any floor were even cracked.

Mira rounded the corner to the back of the hospital. There was a loading bay. The double doors were locked, but they had to get supplies sometime, somehow. She would wait as long as it took.

It was only an hour until a huge truck pulled up. The driver got out and opened the back. It was empty. The double doors of the hospital swung open and Mira slipped behind one of them to be out of sight.

"This isn't a refrigerated truck," a guy on the other side of the door said.

"We're all out" replied the driver.

In a minute, two men she assumed were orderlies started loading bodies on to the truck.

Mira gasped and pressed her hands to her mouth.

The bodies weren't in bags and so Mira held her breath, held her place and watched the faces of the dead until the truck was almost full.

"How many more?" the driver asked.

"As many as you can take."

"Six. I can take six."

"We can get more in."

"No." The driver hung his head in despair. "Six. Have some respect."

The orderlies moved back into the hospital.

Mira sneaked inside. They likely saw her, but no one cared. She made her way down the crowded hall, looking into every face—living and dead.

"Better mask up." Someone pointed to a supply room.

She went inside and put on double masks and gloves.

"Are these all the dead?" she asked.

"For this hour. The rest are gone."

"What happened to them?"

"Cremated. There's too many for anything else."

If Jimmy Rey was dead as Kay said, she had to accept that she would never see him again.

Mira walked down the hall in a daze.

She didn't know how long she put one foot in front of the other, but soon the way looked familiar. She recognized the path to the nurses' station on the floor where she had last left Jimmy Rey and Andee.

"Have you seen them?" Mira asked a nurse she

remembered.

"Honey," she said. "Records went by the wayside a day ago. I can't tell you who has been here or not."

"How are the lists made at the front?"

She shrugged. "Volunteers, I think."

"I can do that," Mira said.

The nurse handed her a legal pad and a pen.

Mira went systematically to every room on that floor. She brought water to the thirsty. Cleaned up vomit from the floor. Held hands and soothed foreheads. And then she moved to the next floor. As she went, she asked about people's loved ones – who was sick and who had died. She did more than make a list of names. She wrote down their stories.

Mira stayed through the night. She escaped in the morning. Jimmy Rey, Andee and Dottie were nowhere to be found. She saw Kay sitting on the curb not far from where Mira had left her. All she did was shake her head.

Kay shuffled to her feet. No answer was not enough.

"I checked every room. I never saw her," Mira said. "They're taking the dead to be cremated every hour."

Kay nodded and stared at her through glassy eyes. Kay was clearly more sick.

"You can get in by the loading dock in the back. Maybe you should go see if there is any help for you."

Kay laid out on the sidewalk.

"I can help you around," Mira said.

Kay shook her head and curled into a fetal position on the ground. Mira stayed with Kay until the end. She stroked Kay's hair and told her stories of Andee.

"I loved her like a sister and a best friend."

After Kay died, Mira thought about telling the orderlies, but she thought that was likely purposeless. In the end, she left Kay where she lay.

Mira took her pages of notes to the television station.

"Is Rory around?" Mira knew that this was the first name of her friend Isa's boyfriend, the newscaster.

"He's on air," the receptionist answered.

"Will you give these to Rory? Maybe he can help with the lists of the dead?" Mira was having difficulty handing them over to the receptionist.

"I can make a copy for you."

"No. Thanks." She realized the futility of this. She went to her apartment to sleep. She fell into her bed and curled up.

Chapter 43 – *Mira* - Sunday, May 3, 2026

Mira was numb, exhausted, but couldn't fall sleep. She wasn't sure she wanted to, except that she wanted to shut off her mind and that wasn't happening. She got up. She couldn't release herself from the two years she had spent isolated from COVID and grieving her father in this same tiny apartment.

She drank a cup of coffee as she emptied the cupboards of any non-perishable food and filled any container with a sealed lid with water. It didn't seem like much.

Mira loaded up her car with the belongings in her apartment. She packed clothes, sheets, dishes and flashlights with batteries. She left behind her schoolbooks. She also left her mother's glass-top desk and her father's overstuffed chair and that made her sadder than she already had been.

The grocery store looked even less approachable than the hospital had, so she didn't even try. She went to Andee's apartment and let herself in. Mira sat down on Andee's couch, completely out of motivation, sapped of her life force. She turned on the television. Red-haired Rory Burke from KNUS was interviewing a scientist who was labeled as Kolli Veddka, Ph.D. in the lower third, but whom Rory called Ved. This was Isa's boyfriend and Isa's father. Mira tried to call the station to see if Isa was there, but no one answered.

"The world has long since reached its tipping point and will no longer be able to support its inhabitants. For too long, we have lived beyond the resources available to us. We keep imagining that the end would be in the distant future, but it's not. The end is now."

Rory turned to camera, explaining, "So, the idea of this group of wealthy men called the Darwins was to hole up in well-stocked resorts while much of the world's population died off, thereby leaving enough of everything for those left behind."

"Yes, but they wanted to speed things up," Ved answered. "The plan wouldn't work if we were like a crab in a pot of water slowly brought to a boil. Crabs have to be thrown into boiling water. They wanted to control the cook."

"Hence they created this deadly and fast-moving virus."

"Yes."

"Ved, might this have worked in theory?"

"Well, I think we have the answer to that. They couldn't control it. They died from it. Between natural and man-made disasters, the current estimate is that half of the world's population will die in less than a year, most in this hemisphere."

Mira groaned and slumped down on Andee's sofa.

"These twenty or so men made fortified resorts they called "hives" for themselves, their families and maybe a chef or maid or two," Rory said. "These men seeking control over us all were wealthy business owners, politicians and leaders in our society."

"History shows us what a few evil people in the right place at the right time can bring," Ved said. "Their only goal seemed to be to make themselves richer and more powerful humans."

The two men stared at each other for a moment beating back feelings too strong to let loose.

"What do we know about how many and where these hive places might be?" Rory asked.

Fancy resorts with high walls, Mira thought. Things were beginning to make sense.

"Nothing. We have no idea." Ved said.

"They kept their secrets well."

"Yes, but these men had always been wealthy. I don't think they thought through the world they would leave behind. I don't think they considered the skill sets of all the others who would die," Ved said. "What happens when the farmers die? The tin can makers? The chocolatiers. What will happen to these people and their high-life then? Even if they survive the pandemic, how can they restart?"

"We received word this morning that the virus has run rampant through the hydro-electric plant. Access to water will end soon," Rory reported, "followed by electricity."

"Yes. That's the way it's expected to go. First people and then utilities and infrastructure and then communications. We're lucky that Wi-Fi, the Internet and broadcasting has stayed up as long as it has. All will die."

It wasn't clear to Mira whether he meant utilities or people — or cleverly worded for both.

"So, what do you recommend we do now?" Rory asked Ved.

"Live as best you can for as long as you can. Take care of yourself and your neighbors. Love someone."

Rory's turned to camera. His smile was sad. "I'm here to bring you the news for as long as I can."

The screen went blank. Mira clicked off the broadcast.

She went through Andee's pantry and picked up some more food and water. She took Jimmy Rey's toolbox. She saw that it contained a couple rolls of duct tape. Good. She grabbed his spare work boots and several pairs of socks that might make them fit better. She packed books, mostly the paperback detective novels that Andee liked to read. She could think of nothing else that might make holing up in her cabin more livable—except people.

She spotted a photo of Jimmy Rey and Andee on a bookshelf. She picked it up and mumbled, "Love someone." She put the photo into her bag.

Mira hadn't given up all hope. She hadn't seen a body or a name on a list. Just in case, she wrote Andee a note. *Come to the land if you can. I love you.*

Chapter 44 – *Mira* – Sunday, May 3, 2026

The spring had been a parched one leaving the ground gasping for water. Temperatures had been over one hundred degrees for much of March and April. There had been only a few spring showers, these replaced with sudden and violent dry storms. The wind kicked up on Mira's drive back to the land and dark clouds formed overhead. As she got close, the sky bombarded the ground with columns of lightening, but any rain evaporated before it reached the ground – dry lightning – and then the boom.

Mira pulled into the parking lot at the cabin. There were two cars: Jayson's SUV and the white Camry that had chased her at the lab. The Camry was parked at the far end of the lot. She stared at it for a minute. It didn't scare her anymore. Maybe, she would infect whoever owned the car and he would die.

Jayson's SUV was parked near where she pulled in, but there was no evidence of Jayson or anyone else. With the next lightning strike, boom. The far hill near where the barrel of crude oil was found exploded.

She leaned forward and grabbed the dashboard. She caught a glimpse of white at the top of the hill, a bright spot on the horizon moving at a steady pace. It took a second to process. She sucked in her breath. In a few more seconds, she saw it again. Her heart pounded. She couldn't breathe. Smoke. Fire.

If Jimmy Rey had been here, he would have likely put it out. He had dug fire ditches and set up fire stations with extinguishers and pails to bring water from the river, but Jimmy Rey was no longer here. It was up to her. She got out of the car and walked into a field with patches of wilting bluebonnets. She was alone surrounded by spots of blue and purple that stretched for a couple acres in every direction. *I'm going to die alone,* she thought.

A moment's peace was shattered by the crack of lightning and then a resounding boom. Mira crushed her body down to the ground. When nothing further happened, she lifted her eyes from the flowers and leaves where she had made a smashed place. She stuck to the earth for a minute, sitting cross-legged and thinking about her predicament. Catastrophe was close.

When she rose, she saw a pillar of fire in the distance. It was behind the tall hill on the other side of the Firebrand River. It soared skyward and then spread into a looming cloud of gray that covered the top of the nearby berm. Fire capped the top of the high hill—a bright line with the colors of a perfect sunset. The fire dripped like orange paint down the slope toward her.

"Jayson," she yelled at the top of her lungs, but got no response. "Fire," she managed to scream even louder, but her warning was likely buried under a roar of growing intensity.

Mira watched the flames climb a tree on the side of the hill. In one minute, the front of the hill ignited. It became an inferno rising into the sky and scorching the earth. Mira sweltered in the sudden heat.

Riley ran by her. She hadn't even seen him arrive. He crossed the field at full speed and splashed into the river, swimming toward the other side. He began to flounder about half way across, his arms waving in the air.

Mira followed Riley. She barreled across the field and into the water. She grabbed a paddleboard, pulled herself on top, grabbed an oar and started paddling.

"What are you doing?" she yelled as she approached

him. "Are you insane?" She was wet through and shivering, whether from panic or the chill water she didn't know.

That's when she saw him – Jayson. As she watched, he fell to the ground on the distant shore overtaken by smoke and heat. Mira sat down on the paddleboard to make it more stable as she pulled Riley onto it. She paddled toward Jayson.

Jayson was burned on both arms. His eyes were swollen and closed. He opened them a slit, saw her and whispered her name. He coughed as his breathing grew ragged.

Fire surrounded them on both sides of the river. It ate the dry fodder that covered the land. She fell to her knees as she watched their escape route combust and turn into Hell.

Both she and Riley slid off the paddleboard. Riley dragged Jayson more securely onto it. Riley took off his shirt and dipped it into the river. He placed his shirt over Jayson's nose and mouth.

"He can't take breathing in any more of this smoke and ash," Riley said. "We can float down the river for a ways.

"Good thinking," Mira said, but she was wondering *then what?* They couldn't get to a car to drive for help. They couldn't get Jayson into the hospital even if they got there.

Jayson grasped her wrist. He slapped at the shirt over his mouth, so Mira removed it. "No. No. Up. About half a mile up river. My name and code 69315."

"69315," Mira said, but she wasn't really paying attention.

"Say it again." Jayson's voice was weak.

"69315," Mira repeated.

"If we go upriver, we have to paddle against the flow. It will be harder," Riley said.

"Upriver," Jayson whispered.

"Yeah, but we should go," Mira said to Riley. "He knows something we don't."

In her mind, she said the numbers again. It had to be a code for a car or a house. Something.

Riley just shrugged. He moved to one side of the paddleboard and began kicking. Mira moved to the other.

Chapter 45 – *Mira* - Sunday, May 3, 2026

Mira saw the tall wall. It was finished and now looked impenetrable and foreboding. The fire had reached it and, finding nothing to burn, had moved on. The earth up to it was scorched and black, but the sky on the other side was mostly blue—no smoke. Riley walked off to follow the wall. Mira stayed with Jayson.

Riley peeked his head around a corner. "Gate," he called to her as he walked back to her side.

She picked up one end of the paddleboard and Riley lifted the other.

"You know he's dead, right?"

"We'll bury him," Mira said. "If there's a place. Save his watch and his ring for his mother."

"You know the watch stopped working in the water," Riley said.

"Maybe a jeweler can fix it. Later. After it dries out."

They reached a massive gate and Mira punched in the code—69315.

"Name," an automated system came back.

"Jayson Brookshire," she said.

"Name print saved."

Great. She was Jayson Brookshire.

The heavy gate slid open. They stepped through and the gate slid shut and locked behind them. Mira wondered if they would be locked inside when the power went out as Isa's father had promised, but then she saw the solar panels on the gate and another wide array on the lawn. This place would have electricity long after it was gone most everywhere else.

On this side of the gate was heaven: trees, grass, flowers in neatly organized beds that looked like an English garden. Along the inside wall on one side of the gate were raised beds filled with milkweed and covered with monarch butterflies that the milkweed attracted. On another length of wall were bee hives. In the distance, Mira could see a glass-sided building with a tennis court inside.

Mira and Riley looked at each other and then took their tattered and soaked selves up to the Welcome Center. It was sun-soaked and cozy-warm, outside and in. They left Jayson on a bench under a portico outside the front door.

In a wide foyer, Mira hit a touch pad and looked up Jayson's name. He was assigned to Hut Two. The kiosk spit out a key.

The "hut" was a three-bedroom, two bath house that was larger than any place she had ever lived, even her mother's huge house. It had floor to ceiling windows in the front room and an accordion door leading to a lanai that overlooked a community pool. Five similar houses surrounded the pool.

"I'm going to take a look around, see who's here," Riley said.

Mira nodded and watched as he went to the house next door and knocked. There was no answer.

Mira went into Jayson's house.

There was a fully stocked pantry in the kitchen. She found a bag of rice, poured some into a bowl and covered Jayson's watch and her phone with it. Maybe that would help to dry them out.

Mira walked from room to room, taking in the transitional furniture design that was both sleek and comfortable.

After a few minutes, Riley bobbed in. "This is so cool."

"Come on," Mira said. "Let's find a shovel and a place

for Jayson. Maybe in that garden."

Chapter 46 – *Mira* – Saturday, May 9, 2026

Mira spent her first six days watching the world fall apart on a sixty-five-inch television. She lay on the couch under a blanket and shivered even though she was certain it wasn't chilly in the house. They had turned on the HVAC.

Riley swam in the pool and gorged on junk food. He seemed to be having a grand time. The fire still smoldered outside the gate, dying in one spot and starting up elsewhere. At any moment, the gate to the outside might be impassable. Mira pulled her phone from the rice, fiddled with it for a minute, but it didn't work. Internet connectivity had been sporadic and the T.V. promised it would get worse.

They had a well-stocked pantry, refrigerator, freezer and movie theatre. Electricity from the outside came with rolling black-outs. The main power grid could fail at any moment, but she wasn't worried. They had generators and solar panels.

Mira had hardly eaten for the two days. She should get up and have some cereal or something, but she didn't have the energy.

Riley was obsessed with the arcade. "Play with me. Play with me," he whined.

Riley had been a big help with burying Jayson. He'd turned out to be useful in his adult moments, but he straddled a shifting line between man and child.

Plus, he'd developed this last man and woman on earth fantasy in his head. He kept trying to have sex with her. He seemed to think he could wear her down, but he was getting on her very last nerve. The television said it might be months, maybe years, before they could come out of quarantine. She couldn't be alone with Riley for years.

She did some counting in her head.

"Where are your parents?" Mira asked Riley.

"Already dead, car accident," he said.

"And your friends? Do you have a special friend?"

He looked at her with hurt eyes. "You," he said.

"Alrighty then." Mira went under the covers to think for a minute. When she came out, Riley was still staring at her with puppy dog eyes. She fiddled with her phone for a bit longer, and then said, "Okay. Arcade it is."

The next morning, Mira opened the gate.

"What are you doing?" Riley asked.

"I want to invite some people to join us," she said. "This place will hold at a minimum twenty-four people. We need to share."

"This is our place," Riley got sulky.

"It's still our place."

The fire was raging, but it had moved into the distance. Both the river and the road seemed accessible.

Riley closed the gate. "Anyone we invite in should quarantine for at least three days. That's what I heard on the TV—three days was generous."

"Let's use the Welcome Center for that."

"Naw. No way. They come in after they quarantine."

"I see the advantage of keeping the walled in space pristine, but how do you propose we do that?"

"I saw some party canopies in the storage building. We put them up outside, label them Day One, Day Two and Day Three. We give them food, water and blankets."

"And what, they sleep on the ground?"

"You're already getting spoiled by our new digs. People who come out to camp sleep on the ground every weekend."

Mira smiled. "True."

Mira helped Riley to erect the canopies. They moved some lawn chairs under the tarps. They found a couple of ice chests and filled them with canisters of water. Mira left Riley to hang bags of food from the tent poles and set up the beds.

Mira put the paddleboard on top of a golf cart she found in a huge underground garage. She followed the road around toward her property. She had put hers, Jayson's and Riley's keys into her shoulder bag in case one of the cars was missed by the fire. She paddled back across the river. Sitting on the gravel lot, strangely, they all were.

Mira's car was filled with her belongings, so she left it in the lot and took Jayson's SUV. She drove into town on deserted streets.

Mira went to the police station. It looked open, so she put on a face mask and went inside. No one sat at the desk. She guessed that wasn't a good use of time at this point. She wondered the halls until she found a person.

"I'm trying to find Detective Walt Liskin." Mira asked.

"I don't think anyone is working in the building except dispatch. They might be able to get in touch with him." The officer pointed down the hall.

An officer in dispatch set her up with a walkie and put her through to Walt. "You know those hives they talk about on the news," Mira said. "I've found one. Comfortable, fully stocked. It was designed for about twenty-four people and I'm going at least two more places, but I'm not turning anyone away." Mira went on to explain the situation and she gave Walt detailed directions. "Everyone will have to quarantine at least three days outside the gate. We're setting it up as best we can. Come tomorrow at ten in the morning."

She'd hung up the phone, but called Walt right back.
"Is Miles still in town?"
"Yes, he's staying with his mother."
"Please bring them."

Chapter 47 – *Mira* – Saturday, May 9, 2026

Mira drove around empty neighborhoods in a fog and ended up on campus. School was closed due to the flu outbreak. Sidewalks, and she assumed the whole campus, were deserted. She parked her car and walked.

The three people who were there wore double surgical masks over their noses and mouths. Mira put on her N95 mask. Of the three people, two were covered up, all except her friend.

"Spooky, huh?" Isa asked.

Mira sat on the low wall next to Isa Vedkka. Isa looked worn with the bags of a seventy-year-old under her eyes.

Today was supposed to be graduation day for Isa. Next Wednesday was law school graduation day for her. Mira guessed that Isa was feeling devastated, just as she was, at the ways their lives had gone off track. Mira took this quiet moment to say good-bye to all her dreams. It felt selfish when she had lost so much more, but she needed it. She needed to take a moment to recognize that her life would never be the same.

"The dean of students insists that graduation is only being postponed," Isa said "but I don't believe it."

"Guess I'm not going to be a lawyer," Mira said.

"Guess I'm not going to be an artist," Isa replied.

"You still could," Mira said. "To think just a few weeks ago we were talking about our future. What type of law I would practice. Where I would find a job. I didn't tell you that I got an offer in Memphis. Guess I'm not going there."

"I was talking about what galleries might take my art."

Impulsively, Mira leaned over and pulled Isa into her

arms. They held each other for only a moment.

"Thanks," Isa said. "I needed that."

"I was sorry to read in the newspaper about the death of your mother," Mira said. "The paper wasn't very clear on what happened."

"She was murdered," Isa said with wet eyes.

Mira waited to see if Isa wanted to say more, but she didn't. "I tried to come by to see you, but, as it turns out, I don't have your address."

"I guess our friendship has mostly happened on this wall," Isa said. "I wanted to call too, but I didn't have your contact information either."

"I did come to the memorial," Mira said. "It was really special."

"I wish I'd seen you there."

"I didn't wish to intrude," Mira said. Tears welled in her eyes.

Mira saw the red-haired reporter from KNUS walking toward them. Rory smiled and Mira noticed that he was not wearing a mask either.

It dawned on Mira then. Isa's mother was a scientist. She had been part of the twenty-two scientists who were murdered in their lab. Rory Burke covered the story. " She took Isa's hand. "I recently went to see him at the station, but didn't get further than reception. I'm glad Rory made it."

Isa put her arm around Mira again and they sat in silence thinking of people gone from them and all they had lost.

"Hello," Mira said as Rory reached them and sat on the other side of Isa.

"Hi," Rory said. "You should know, I've started a new sequence."

"How can you," Isa asked. "Wi-Fi has gone out."

"Got someone working on that. She thinks she can get WiFi back up, at least for as long generators and power packs hold out for listeners. I've also found a CB radio at the station. Good one. Old school. I'm thinking that once a day I'll send out all the news that's fit to air."

Mira was thinking that she had seen one of those in the office at the Welcome Center. She could listen in.

"Why should I know you've started something new?" Mira asked.

"Because you were the inspiration. I'm taking your lists to start, finding out all I can about those people and doing a memorial for each as I can. I'm hoping other people will send me more memories of more people."

Mira broke into tears. "Can I tell you about my best friends Andee and Jimmy Rey?"

Rory pulled a notebook and a pen from a pocket. "I'd love to hear about them."

And so Mira did.

Isa twined her fingers with Mira's and turned to look at her.

"Before my mother died," she said, "she developed a vaccine for this flu that's going around. It's not yet released to the public, so we haven't said anything to the public, but it's safe. My father is working with the CDC to get it out to everyone."

Isa pulled down Mira's mask. "Do you remember a day when we were sitting right here and I sprayed a puff of air from a canister into your face."

"I think I do," Mira said.

"That was the test vaccine. You might have felt punk for a day, but now you're immune."

"What? Really?" Mira gagged thinking about the people who were already lost and the many more that may come. She wasn't sure being vaccinated was a blessing.

"I had to make hard choices," Isa said. "There wasn't enough vaccine. I couldn't save everyone."

Mira didn't envy Isa those choices, but she felt awash with pain and guilt. Why should she get to live while Jimmy Rey and Andee did not?

"They're working on making the vaccine available to the everyone, but that will take a while. After my mother died, my father shared her work on the formula with the scientific community around the world and that saved some time. They," she said with finger quotes around the word, "are rushing testing through, but there are still approvals, manufacturing and distribution. This flu moves so fast and is so deadly, millions, maybe billions, of people will die before that's done."

"At least something's started," Mira said. "I hope it's not like COVID-19 where so many people refused to take it that the virus hung on and on."

"We don't have to worry about deniers," Rory responded. "Anybody who refuses to take this vaccine will be dead by next year no matter how many precautions they try to take."

Mira was shocked at the harsh words. She wanted to say that it would all be okay, but she didn't believe that herself. "The world has ended," Mira repeated what Andee's mom said and Rory mirrored.

Mira got up, leaned down, and gave Isa a kiss on her cheek. "You can come the hive, if you wish."

"We have a safe place to hole up." Isa said.

"If you change your mind, come anytime." She handed Isa a paper with directions.

"We won't," Rory said. "We have stuff to do."

"You know what I've learned from all this," Isa said. "If it just takes a few people to bring this much bad into the world, it doesn't take any more to bring as much good."

Mira walked away before they could see the tears streaming down her face.

Chapter 48 – *Mira* – Sunday, May 10, 2026

In the morning, Mira waited outside the gate. Mira had wondered how she got out of the hospital alive when she'd gone looking for her friends. She should have been dead three times over. Now she understood why not. That vaccine worked well.

She told Riley about the vaccine last night. They agreed she would do all interaction with the people in quarantine. He was okay with that.

After a while, a car pulled in. Nathan Roget tumbled out of the car. That was wonderful. Maddox and Nathan looked like just the sort of boy-company that Riley needed. She didn't have phone numbers for many of the volleyball players, but Walt was able to call some of the regulars.

Next, Walt showed up with his wife and twin girls, both nineteen with long, silver-white hair. If she thought Riley would be happy before.... Mira let that thought wander. There was also a woman Mira had assumed was Walt's mother, but he introduced her as Tula Guzman.

"She's a forensic accountant," he said. "She was on your team."

"Welcome," Mira said.

A couple more cars arrived and then it was quiet for a long time. Mira helped people get settled and then started a list of things they might need from inside the gates.

A final car came slowly up the drive at sunset. Mira smiled with relief as Miles stepped out of the car. A woman, mid to late forties, followed.

"This is my mother, Geri," he said.

"It's nice to meet you," Mira said.

Miles turned to look at her. "Jimmy Rey?" he asked.

Mira shook her head. "Andee too." Her voice cracked with grief.

Miles pulled her into his chest and stroked her hair. She took a breath, maybe the first one since the last time she saw him. Her arms went around his waist.

Chapter 49 – *Mira* - Tuesday, May 19, 2026

It took eight days before they were ready to let people out of quarantine. They lost two people along the way. Each time someone got sick, they started quarantine over again.

They started a little cemetery outside the gates. Riley dug up a small tree to transplant and some flowers from the garden. He also found some spare garden stakes and burned the names of each person into them. Mira picked up the items at the gate and everyone helped with the digging.

Finally, Mira opened the gates and let everyone see their new home. They were stunned to see living trees and flowers, bees and butterflies. It was beautiful, especially considering the ash and char they had been breathing for days. It was like Oz—color for the first time. They stood at the gate unable to move forward.

"Come on," Mira said. She beckoned with her fingers.

"Are you sure we're allowed?" Walt asked.

"We were invited," Mira assured him.

"It looks like peace," Tula smiled.

Mira introduced Riley. "Assign them a house and show them around." Riley had systematically broken all the locks in the hive for places they could not enter. "Show them the pool and the arcade," Mira said.

"There's a pool?" Maddox said. He started the rush into the compound.

Mira hadn't told Riley about Maddox, Nathan or the twins. He was suddenly happy, as she knew he would be, as he closed and locked the gate behind them and led the way.

"Let's set up a bar-b-que by the pool tonight," Mira said.

"Yeah," Riley said. "Let's have a party."

It was decided that Miles and Geri would move in with Mira and Riley. Tula moved in as well. Mira thought this was going to work out just fine.

Later, the three boys were splashing in the water. The two girls sat poolside ignoring them. The boys' mother, Juliette, came over to say hello to Miles and Geri. Mira didn't ask why Juliette's husband wasn't with them. Just like she didn't ask Miles where Tina and Cal were.

Tula pulled Geri and Juliette right into the action. "I'm making potato salad. Come help."

Around sunset, a family of seven joined them at the pool. Mira didn't know the newbies. *How did they get inside?* Mira wondered. Mira walked over. "Hi. I'm Mira Ashe."

"I saw that you used Jayson's code," the father said. I'm a friend of Jayson. Is he here?

Mira shook her head.

"Can you tell me what happened to him?"

I'm sorry to say that Jayson died in the fire outside. Riley and I brought him here. I'll show you where he's buried tomorrow if you like."

"I'm so sorry to hear that. He was a good guy. I liked him very much."

"How did you know Jayson?"

"He worked for me. I'm Trey Andover and this is my wife and five little girls."

"Will there be more," Riley asked from the shallow end of the pool.

"More people who know the code like I do?" Trey said. "I don't think so. I was supposed to release the code at the right time to all the families who had paid. I didn't do that. I can't do that. I don't know who they are."

"Riley," Mira said. "More people will come. Word will get out."

"Yes," Trey said. "I'm surprised to not see more of the construction workers. I would have thought they would have made their way out to the gate."

Mira nodded.

"Well, that's a problem for another day," Riley said.

It grew late and bugs were out, so everyone moved into the pool's clubhouse. At nine o'clock, Mira stood and turned on the television.

"Hi all," Rory Burke said over the air waves. I'm sorry to say that this will be our last television broadcast. This is our last generator and it's going fast. We hope that we can find sufficient petrol to stay on the air for the next hour. After tonight we will be broadcasting the news on CB radio at this same hour."

Rory gave the audience all the information to stay in touch. Mira didn't need it; she had been in contact with them already. Many times.

"On Sundays at ten o'clock in the morning, we will also introduce a special CB broadcast that we will conduct each week. It will be a memorial, a remembrance of loved ones that we lost. This Sunday will be the first one and it's a special thanks to our friend Mira Ashe."

"Jimmy Rey," Miles said and Mira nodded yes. "And Andee."

"And her mother, Kay, and Dottie from the store," Mira said. "Plus, Jayson Brookshire who we all have to thank for this sanctuary."

"First the news," Rory continued, "We have long wondered why these men chose to do this awful thing. Well, we have something new to share," Rory said. "I was recently provided with this." He held up a flash drive. "It's a video that was taken at a picnic in the year 2012. There was no sound at the time, but narration was recently added."

Rory clicked a few buttons on his computer and a grainy home surveillance video began. Outside a window, party guests cooked on the grill or played in the pool. The view switched to a man standing at the window.

"That's Bertram Wagner of the Wagner Company—a major pharmaceutical enterprise," said an unknown voice. "This is his house. Bertram was an imposing figure. He took up a lot of space." Bertram Wagner moved to fill a closed, dark oak door on the video. The heavy door opened to a dark and daunting study.

"He's talking to my grandfather, Ansel Andover, the mega construction guy." Ansel was older, skinny, frail-looking. "We called him Number One, like on Star Trek."

Mira cast a glance at Trey. It sounded like his voice.

"They called my dad Junior. He died the year before this was filmed in what they called the 2011 Super Tornadoes. Dad was driving home from a job site. He was building condos in Tuscaloosa, Alabama when an EF4 tornado hit, catching him and his car and flinging them both miles away. He did not die immediately. It took several days."

The two men on screen made themselves comfortable in overstuffed chairs.

"Bertram is about to turn sixty and Number One is well into his seventies." The narrator paused. "I'm called Trey—Ansel Andover the third."

All eyes in the room turned to Trey.

"Huh," Riley said.

Bertram lit a cigar and Number One gulped an oversized drink.

"You would think given what we know now that Bertram's motivation would have started with the death of his own son, Percy, in the 2023 Tsunami off the Florida Coast. But no, my grandfather picked Bertram because of his wife."

The two men pulled their chairs close and leaned in as they silently conspired.

"When you read about the cause of Penny Wagner's death, it's reported that she died giving birth to twins, Pierce and Percy. What it doesn't say is that Penny was swept up in hurricane Danielle which caused massive flooding in Austin, Texas in 1980. Toxins she was exposed to in the floodwater caused sepsis which is what actually caused her death. "

Number One stood and walked toward the door.

"I was twelve years old when I took this silent film. Even though, there was no sound to remind me, I remember what my grandfather said as he closed the door on me. He said, 'Are you with me? We have got to do something about this weather.'"

Trey picked up the buttons for the television and turned off the sound. "It's amazing the harm that two old, wealthy and angry men can cause just by sulking together in a dark room," he said.

Mira thought of what Isa had said. It was pretty much the same thing, expect she added to it. "If two old men can bring so much bad into the world, think how much good all of us can bring."

Part IV

Chapter 50 – *Alonzo* - March 2003

Texas City made a stinky introduction to the Gulf coast and the island of Galveston. The suburb of Houston was known for its deep-water port and railways, but that's not where the smell originated. Its numerous smoke-belching, petro-chemical plants fouled the air.

Alonzo Rossi went to work as night manager when the lights brightened the sky like a Christmas tree. The Origin Oil Refinery was running two consecutive shifts in order to meet a ridiculous deadline. Even with overtime, Lonny barely made enough money to pay his bills. It wasn't worth the hard, long hours.

Oil refineries had accidents on boats, on drilling rigs and on land. Most were big, full of fire and smoke, and hard to miss, but not all. Lonny was ready to move on from this job.

To beef up staffing, Origin had hired fifteen contractors to supplement the regular staff on the two shifts. Origin rented and installed four cheap trailers as housing for the contractors on site. The outside of each trailer had the oval shape of an oversized Tylenol caplet. Inside, each trailer was a hollow home for two guys, yet four men shared each—two on the day shift and two on the night shift. There were a pair of stacked bunk beds, a small sitting area and a tiny kitchen.

Lonny got a call from his buddy Carlton Ashe, whom he called Cash, to come to trailer B. The sickly-sweet smell of rotten eggs grew stronger filling the air as he moved closer. Lonny went to the nearest safety box and pulled out a couple gas masks and gloves.

Cash's truck was parked between a storage unit and

trailer B. Six barrels were loaded onto the truck bed and one sat on the ground. A dark liquid made a small wet spot under it.

Cash pushed open the door to the trailer and put a finger to his lips. "Don't say a word," Cash said. "It's not my fault. I swear."

Lonny raised his palm to stop Cash from jabbering.

Lonny and Cash were in the process of stealing six barrels of refined oil. They got paid two hundred dollars a barrel each time they transported them – twelve hundred bucks.

It was supposed to be simple. Mealtime, the quietest part of the night. Lonny would let Cash drive on site and then he would open the storage area that contained the barrels of oil. After that, Lonny would go eat with his team. Cash would switch empty barrels with the full ones, load them onto his truck and cover them with a tarp. After the food break, Lonny would open the gate and Cash would drive the truck out. Lonny would leave in the morning when his shift was over.

"How many full barrels you got on the truck?" Lonny asked.

"All six," Cash replied.

"So, what's this?" Lonny pointed to a seventh barrel.

"An extra. It was just sitting there by the trailer."

"So, you just thought you would take it."

"Sure, why not?"

Lonny pointed to a sticker on the side. "Because it's toxic sour crude, not refined. That's why not." *Proper security was a joke at Origin*, Lonny thought. A guy who did not work here got onsite and picked up a barrel of toxic, sour crude. He could feel it already. Somehow, he would be blamed for this.

Crude oil was a mixture of fluids, gases and

contaminants. Crude oil with a high sulfur content was called "sour." It could emit hydrogen sulfide or H2S at any point in processing, at wellheads, pumps, piping, separation devices, water storage vessels and oil storage tanks. If not immediately needed, it was supposed to be stored in salt caves in atmospheric pressure containers. Additives should be mixed with the oil to prolong shelf life and make it more stable, but these were often not added or they degraded over time.

Cash was normally fit and lean, but right now he looked bloated and his face was an unnatural shade of red. He was also freaked out.

Lonny gave Cash a gas mask. "Put this on and keep it on," he said. "It's important."

Lonny stepped inside the trailer. The lights were off, but the windows provided enough light that Lonny could see that two bunks were full.

Lonny checked his H2S detector. It was too high, way too high. There was hydrogen sulfide in the air.

"Hey, rise and shine, assholes," Lonny said as he looked toward Cash.

"I don't think they'll be doin' that," Cash said as he backed up a few steps.

"What are you talking about?" Lonny poked the guy sleeping nearest to him, but the guy didn't move, didn't wake, and didn't breathe.

"I was moving the extra barrel to the truck when I noticed the top wasn't tight and it was leaking."

"Fumes?" Lonny asked. Hydrogen sulfide was a colorless, corrosive and poisonous gas could be rapidly absorbed into the lungs. "It stinks. That's the sweet smell."

"Didn't they smell it?" Cash asked.

"Sense of smell is first to go. Death can come really fast after that."

Cash jabbed the body. "Damn. What are we going to do?"

Lonny plopped on the sofa and thought. Cash jabbered the whole time in a frenzy of meaningless words, but Lonny had a plan.

"The refinery is poorly maintained," Lonny said. "Safety equipment is faulty and alarms break all the time. The big bosses are gonna need a scapegoat for this. All my back due reports will be enough to put me in jail for a lifetime. We got to get these bodies out of here."

One of the main parts of his job at the refinery was ensuring safety and efficiency, but that was nearly impossible with the demands of management and the budget he had do it. Trouble was inevitable.

Lonny loaded the seventh barrel onto the bed of Cash's truck. He hooked up the trailer with the two dead bodies in it to his truck and they drove into the night.

Chapter 51 – *Alonzo* **- March 2003**

The truck roared down the highway, Lonny at the wheel—its bed filled with the clanking of the barrels. Cash sat in the passenger seat and coughed. For almost an hour, Lonny and Cash argued about what to do with the trailer and its contents. Lonny was in favor of getting rid of the trailer as soon as possible. He wanted to get Cash to a doctor. Cash didn't look too good and Lonny was worried about him.

"I got a place in mind," Cash whispered between hacks. "Let's go to the drop-off. It's near there. I'll go to my doctor tomorrow."

After hours of driving, Lonny turned the truck onto a deserted two-lane, eventually reaching an old filling station. Behind the station was a ramshackle barn.

Cash gave Lonny a key to unlock a padlock on the barn. In the barn was a forklift and a front loader. Lonny used the forklift to pull the barrels off the truck and transfer them to a pad near the fuel pumps. On one end of the pad was a 550 gallon above-ground heavy duty tank. The pad and the tank were under an aluminum car port cover to protect the tank from heat or hail.

Lonny watched while Cash sent a text to a number, he knew not where. When Cash got home, twelve hundred dollars would be in his account and Cash would split that with him.

It was about three o'clock in the morning when Lonny and Cash arrived at their second stop.

"What is this place?" Lonny asked.

"End-of-the-worlders bought land to build a posh resort. Condos for about twenty or thirty rich people.

Tennis court. Putting green. A swimming pool. My job is helping them stock up. That's what the oil's for." That was more words than Cash had said in an hour, so he punctuated it with a coughing fit. Lonny slapped him on the back like that would help.

"What are they worried about? This place won't be much use in a nuclear war."

"I think it's germs. They're preparing for the next great pandemic."

"You gonna live here at the end-times?" Lonny asked smirking.

"You have to pay a million dollars to get on a list. I haven't got that," Cash said. "The survivalists think I don't know where they're building, but a short morning of following the pickup from here to the construction crew took care of that."

Lonny got Cash a bottle of water from a small ice chest behind the driver's seat and left him in the cab of the truck to rest while Lonny took care of things.

The ground had been leveled in places and dirt pushed by heavy equipment into hills of loose earth. Lonny parked the trailer with the bodies near another trailer that served as an office for the construction crew. There was a lockbox on the trailer door that Lonny smashed. He grabbed the keys to the backhoe-loader.

Cash pointed to a nice spot that was near the edge of the river. It was lined with trees. "On the plans, this spot isn't scheduled to be anything other than pretty." There was a rise—a hill of dirt—that ran along the shore. Lonny got an angle on it and began ripping the top of the hill off. After a couple hours, he had turned the hill into a hole that was at least seven feet deep.

Lonny loaded each dead man from the trailer into the loader and transported them to the hole. He felt bad. He didn't want to just dump these two men into the blackness. He knew them. He liked them, but he saw no alternative. He released the loader and down they went.

He pushed the rich, black soil onto them until the hill looked somewhat the same size as before. The construction crew wouldn't be back for a few weeks—maybe a couple months. They didn't know it, but it was Cash who had been the cause of their permit issues. With some luck, maybe Cash could think of a way to delay the permits further.

Lonny made another indention into the side of the hill. Carefully, wearing mask and gloves, Lonny used the forklift to move the barrel from the back of the truck. He covered it with a tarp and then returned the dirt. He did it by himself as Cash was too weak to help.

The dark sky was turning hazy as he stood staring at the trailer. What to do with it? The inside didn't look like a crime scene. Two men had just refused to wake up. He decided to just leave trailer B where it was. Lonny opened all the windows. He pulled the men's few belongings and loaded them into his truck, wiping surfaces as he went. He removed all ID from the trailer like plates and registration papers. He left the door unlocked. He imagined the construction crew finding it and thinking it was a perk from the company—a place to get out of the sun and cool off.

Lonny drove away as fast as he could. He wanted out of there. He took Cash home. He and Cash's little girl got Cash into a sofa.

"Tell your mama to take him to the doctor in the morning," Lonny instructed.

"What happened to my daddy?"

Lonny couldn't think of an answer, so he just walked out.

Lonny dropped all the stuff in the truck at a Goodwill store. While he was there, he picked out some new items for himself from the overflow by the bins.

He stopped at a cheap, rural motel and rented a room using cash. He took a long, hot shower. After the hot water ran cold, he fell on the bed. He needed to sleep, but he could not. He stared at ceiling.

Chapter 52 - *Alonzo* - March 2003

In the morning, as Lonny didn't sleep in a nearby motel, the gas station attendant pulled up to the pad. He put on gloves and a respirator. He pulled off the top of the barrel and syphoned the oil into the tank.

At the bottom of each barrel was a sealed canister full of frozen vials. The attendant pulled out the canisters and put them into a large ice chest. He taped all sides of the top to the bottom.

A black SUV arrived around noon. A big man picked up the ice chest and drove it to a private airport where it was loaded onto a plane.

After landing at Boston, a courier service picked up the ice chest and drove it across town. The ice chest was left on a labs' landing bay. A med tech picked it up and put it on a gurney.

In the lab, a doctor in a white coat opened each canister and pulled the vials of virus and put each in a lot designated for it: Flu, Subtype 1 – 18, Measles, Small Pox, Ebola…

"Where do you think they get this constant flow of antigens?" the doctor asked.

"Does it matter?"

The doctor shrugged it off.

Chapter 53 – *Alonzo* -March 2020

Cash died on a Tuesday—the last day in March. They didn't have a funeral for him because people were isolating from COVID-19. Cash's ex-wife did a little memorial online. It didn't seem like much to celebrate a man's whole life.

Lonny went over to Cash's house to see what he could find out about what was what. He put on a mask and gloves and made up a lie. He went when he knew that Mira would be at school. He didn't think Mira would let him rummage through Cash's paperwork, but Mira's mom just waved him inside and told him to use the back door to leave because it locked automatically. She was on her way to tennis, completely ignoring the warnings about wearing masks and staying apart from each other.

That gave Lonny a couple hours to gently search Cash's whole house, but he spent most of his time in Cash's office. In the files, he found the deed to the house and some bills, but nothing that really interested him. He discovered that Cash's computer was not password protected. That was a bit discouraging as it was unlikely anything really good was on it, but he looked anyway. He found copies of tax returns that clearly much had been left out. He knew because the same things had been left out of his returns. Still, he took photos and sent them to his phone. There was no safe that he could find. Finally, he found a lockbox inside a cardboard storage box inside a closet at the back. He couldn't find a key, so he just took the whole lockbox.

When he got the lockbox home, he busted it open with

a hammer and screwdriver. Inside, he found a driver's license and credit card in a false identity, plus a band around $5,000 in cash and three empty bands. Cash never could hold on to money. Lonny found a little piece of paper with a first name and phone number. There was also a flash drive. Lonny spread the contents of the lockbox out on his dining table.

Lonny opened his computer and plugged in the drive. It contained Cash's research into Andover and Associates, their partners and the resort. Cash had lost his health and ultimately his life to that night in Texas City. Cash wanted to know who had made money off that. And now, Lonny did too. He wanted to know who had been paying Cash.

Lonny examined digital bank records for the account where Cash's employer transferred the money for deliveries. The last transaction stood out. Lonny speculated that, after his health went, Cash made such a fuss with his sole contact that one day $80,000 appeared in Cash's bank account via the same channel that he was paid for delivering oil.

Cash used a bit of that money to hire a private investigator to track the money transfers, but the guy's report indicated that he had found out nothing much about it.

Cash had used the largest chunk of that money to buy the property across the river from where the guys were buried. Lonny had wondered where Cash got the funds for that. He thought it might have been Cash's rich wife, but she was notoriously tight about giving him large sums, likely with good reason.

Lonny stood up and paced around the house for a bit. Cash had cut him out of the pay off. He was angry, but couldn't figure out what good that would do him now.

The investigator hadn't been able to track the money to

a person, but he had found the source. The P.I. followed the contact who led him to the Wagner Company. The Wagner Company made legal drugs. Cash was following the hunch that the Wagner Company also made illegal drugs, but the P.I. had not found any evidence of that. What a worthless sot.

Chapter 54 – *Alonzo* – Sunday, April 26, 2026

Dark clouds streamed lightning that fit his mood. Lonny sat on top of the berm where the two men were buried. He'd come out about once a week since the beginning so long ago. He'd spread grass and wildflower seeds over the turned dirt until it became a pastural picture, much too pretty to dig up for a golf course which they had once threatened. Locals would come out with their babies to take family photos on the hill with the blue bonnets, poppies and Indian paint brush in the background.

On the surface, it seemed that things had been going decently for Lonny in the last couple of decades. He'd been working in real estate for a while now and he'd gotten his broker's license. He'd met a pretty gal named Bonnie and he hoped that would go somewhere good. He had a nice ranch house with some land and a couple horses. What more could he want?

That was simple—not to go to prison for a double murder.

At Origin, late one night, two guys, Henry Lynton and Eitan Boskova, had caught him moving the six barrels of oil out of the storage shed for Cash to pick up at dinner time. Boskova didn't much care, but Lynton was a stand-up guy, honest and trustworthy. Lonny could see it already beginning to eat at him. Lynton would chew on it for a bit, but ultimately wouldn't let it stand. He knew Henry Lynton would mean trouble, likely in the morning when the day manager came to work.

Lonny donned a hazmat suit and moved an empty barrel to the sour crude oil tank and syphoned off about half a barrel. He let the barrel stew for a bit, and then he moved the barrel to outside the window of the trailer where the guys stayed. He tilted its lid and let H2S leak out. There was no air conditioning in the trailers so the guys slept with the windows and doors open. The fumes filled the air, cutting off their sense of smell and poisoning them. He'd killed two good men for an extra six hundred dollars a month. By accident he'd also killed his best friend, Cash. He'd been greedy and that had made him a murderer.

Lonny felt crazy. He'd been crazy for years. At first, after the incident as he liked to call it, he imagined big, beefy guys following him around. Day and night, they were there. Cash knew that they knew what he'd done. They were there to punish him.

Lonny had cleaned out both his bank accounts, packed only what fit into a duffel, and went to work. When the time seemed right, he had gotten into Henry Lynton's car parked in the employee lot and drove off. After several months of hiding out, he thought he'd shaken the beefcake. He sold Lynton's car and took the bus to Austin to start life over.

For the first fifteen years and despite Cash's ill health, Cash had successfully mucked up the resort's plans to build a golf course, nine holes on their land and nine holes on his, with letters of complaint and legal maneuvering under Cash's signature. Cash would not sell or lease the land to build the back nine. Given that, development never came near to the hill at the river's edge.

But then Cash had died. In Cash's will, he had named Lonny as property manager for his land down by the river, but that didn't give Lonny the same legal status as his daughter who was the owner. Lonny wasn't sure how to stop development any more, especially if Mira decided to sell or lease that piece of the property. She was graduating and might move on. And she'd gotten an offer, apparently a good one.

Lonny hadn't realized how much it meant not to be alone in this. He hadn't slept in most of the five years since Cash died. He had a hole in his chest where his stomach used to be. His hair was falling out. Both his father and grandfather had a full head of shiny white hair all their life, but not him.

Lonny put a cigarette in his lips, but didn't light it. He had taken up smoking again. He'd quit years ago, but between the daytime stress and his nightmares, he had to smoke. But not here while he sat on the hill. He had pictures in his head of H2S fumes leaking up from underground from the crude oil barrel exploding into flames.

Lonny had run out of time. He's seen development plans for the land. Work was being done by Andover and Associates in conjunction with partners, the only one of which he knew was the Wagner Company.

The first Ansel Andover died of the flu just a couple months ago. Since Ansel Andover, Jr. had died in an Alabama tornado years before, Junior's son Trey had inherited the family business. And Trey was rushing. He was in a hurry for some reason. It felt like something had happened that moved up his deadline. He seemed obsessed with quickly finishing construction of his resort.

Trey had completed a tall wall around the resort. He seemed to have forgotten about the golf course that was planned to run on both sides of the river. Lonny hoped, but Trey still wanted all the land beside the river, especially Mira's land. For what he could only guess.

Lonny talked it over with the ghosts of the two men buried under him.

At Origin, Eitan had gone to the bars with him on occasion, had a few beers and played darts. They weren't friends really — more occasional buddies.

The other guy kept to himself more. Still Henry Lynton seemed like a good guy. Young. A family man.

Cash's ghost sat with him on the hill sometimes too. He was here with him today.

"Hey. Look. There's your little girl," Lonny told Cash. "Pretty woman now."

Cash didn't talk to him. None of the ghosts in his head talked. They couldn't tell him what they were thinking. They couldn't forgive him.

"What's she doing?" Lonny watched Mira as she walked to the edge of the pool with a basket. He pulled out his binoculars for a clearer look. She was filling bottles. "Looks like she's taking water samples. Why would she be doing that? What do you think?"

Lonny pulled out his phone and called Riley. "Hey Miller. What's going on at the Ashe land? Is something happening with the sale I don't know about?"

"Lots of commotion last weekend," Riley informed him. "One of the players got himself bitten by a cottonmouth and had to be air-lifted to the hospital."

"I heard something about the water," Lonny probed.

"Oh yeah. Little kids had to be pulled from the lagoon and showered off. It's green and the fish have died."

"What caused that? Do they know?"

"Can't say."

"Did that put off the buyer?"

"Can't say that either. Jayson has his marching orders and he's going to pursue the sale until they tell him not to. He can be relentless."

The lagoon was created from a cup shape in the flow of the river. The very berm on which he sat ran into the cup when it rained and the place where the kids jumped into the pond from the rope swing was on the other side of the cup.

"What killed the fish?" Lonny asked ghost Cash. Lonny didn't like the only logical answer. "Barrels leakin', huh?"

A crazy panic set in. They'd find sour crude in the water, and then they'd track its source, and then they'd find the bodies, and then they'd find him.

Lonny hit another number on his phone. No answer, so he left a message. "Hey Jayson, it's Alonzo Rossi. I heard about the poisonous snakes and polluted water on that slice of land on the Firebrand River. I assume that you want me to start looking at other options. Who would want to play golf in that?"

In a minute, a text came back from Jayson. "Trey still wants the land and we're going to get it for him. Doubled my offer today."

Lonny should dig up the bodies and move them, but he saw what the H2S had done to Cash. He decided against that. If only he could convince Mira not to sell, but Andover sent pretty-boy Jayson to convince her to sell and that seemed to be working.

Ghost Cash looked at him with a mixture of fear and hate in his eyes. Clearly, he wanted Lonny to help his daughter.

Lonny thought about maybe talking to Mira - explain about her father's accident and Lonny had helped cover it up to protect Cash and his family. To protect her. Now it was her turn to protect her father's memory.

Mira was heading to her car with the water samples.

Lonny ran to his white Camry and speed down the

road until he was behind her, following her.

Chapter 55 – *Alonzo* - Sunday, April 26, 2026

Lonny followed her to her apartment. He pulled over and waited as she went inside. He sat in his car down the street watching her front door and obsessing on all he had to lose.

He could see it all laid out it in his mind. She would take the water to the lab and they would identify the toxins in it. The police would start an investigation that would lead to him. Mira and her bottles of dirty water presented the most danger he had been in since the incident.

"I'm sorry," he whispered to dead Cash, "but I'm gonna have to get rid of your little girl."

Lonny mopped his forehead. He was in panic-mode. He didn't make good decisions in panic-mode. He knew that about himself.

He saw a guy deliver flowers to her. Not much later, Jayson Brookshire came to her door with a bunch of his own flowers and wine too. Why two bunches of flowers? Lonny thought it was maybe a date, but when Jayson came out in less than an hour, he had no basket with water samples.

Lonny fretted for a couple more hours, until Mira turned out her lights. It would do him no good to cover up two murders by getting caught for a third. He needed a solid plan. Hopefully, one that looked like an accident.

Sometime during the night, Lonny fell asleep and when he woke up, Mira's car was gone. That brought him to life fast. Maybe she was going to class or the library to study.

He got out of the car and checked her doors and windows to see if he could find a way in. He wanted to search her place and see if the water samples were inside, but he could not find a way. He peed on her sidewall because he had to and because he was frustrated. He got back in his car and headed out.

Lonny sighed with relief when he found Mira on campus sitting on a low wall drinking coffee. She was talking to her painter friend-the girl always covered in spots of color. Mira stayed on campus for a couple hours and then went back to her apartment.

Lonny decided she was in for a while, and so he took a chance and went to a nearby convenience store. Lonny hit the bathroom again and washed his face and hands. He bought some coffee, water and snacks. He filled the car with gas. At the counter, he noticed the store owner had a display of COVID-19 masks. Lonny bought a black one.

Mira was just taking off when he got back to her apartment. He'd almost missed her again. He wasn't dumb enough not to realize that this was because of his reluctance to do what he was gonna do.

He followed her onto the highway. He stayed back a few cars-well hidden. Mira was taking her usual route on school days. But then, she turned left instead of right. He sped up a bit and followed.

Where was she going? Lonny felt his heart pounding in his chest. He pulled out his phone and spoke into the microphone feature. "Water analysis labs near me," he said.

Lonny glanced at his display. There was a listing nearby. His ears rushed with blood and he had trouble hearing the answer. She was going to a lab. She was going to have the water tested. If she got there, he'd be done for.

Mira disappeared around a curve. His foot became heavy without him realizing it until he hit the curve and spun dangerously around. He didn't see that Mira had slowed down while he speeded up. His white Camry hit the back of Mira's car and she skidded into the ditch, but didn't roll over.

His first instinct was to flee. He sped down the road, but turned around knowing this was his time. She took off in the other direction.

Mira slowed down as he built sped. *What is she doing?* he wondered. As he began to ease next to her, she turned her front bumper hard into his right, front tire and pushed. She gave it the gas. Rubber burned as she pushed him off the road. He screamed like a little girl as he skidded halfway down the slope.

Mira drove on, stopped, got out of her car and looked back.

He got out of his car too. He was shaking and it felt as if his knees might give. His car was only three years old, but he didn't carry insurance beyond liability. He circled the Camry. His tire shredded. He was angry now.

"You crazy bitch," he yelled.

He ran toward her. He didn't know what he was gonna do if he caught her, maybe strangle her with his bare hands; he was seeing red. She needed to join the guys inside that hill. What was one more ghost after he had already killed three.

Mira got into her car and raced off.

Lonny fought to calm down.

Chapter 56 – *Alonzo* - Sunday, April 26, 2026

After the mauling she gave his car, Lonny had lost track of Mira. He pulled out the bumper with his hands enough to let the wheels turn and then he changed the tire. he drove to all her usual hangs, but did not find her or her car. After about an hour of pulling his hair out, he went home. He couldn't stalk her anymore that day.

Lonny had a three-bedroom, two-bath ranch house that he had built himself with his own two hands on twelve acres of pristine ranch land. He had a barn with four horse stalls housing three horses as well as a stocked pond with a small dock. He swelled with pride each time he drove through the gates of his property, but it was always mixed with a touch of guilt. He knew he wasn't a good man and didn't deserve such happiness.

Bonnie's baby blue truck was home. His breath caught—anxious to see her.

Bonnie came into his life about six months ago. They met in Vegas. She was on vacation and he was at a real estate conference. She wasn't classically pretty, but she had this thick, long hair that was the color of rust. When he first saw her, she was laying by the pool at the hotel. Her hair shined in the sun with reds, oranges and gold. And then she hit him with that smile. It knocked him over.

Lonny had to wonder what Bonnie would think if she knew about his murderous intent. Bonnie wasn't prim or strict, but she had a strong moral compass. Integrity, she called it. She found honor in truth and amity in helping her community.

She ran a food truck that made fish or chicken tacos and sold them in a park by the convention center. The spot was close to the Salvation Army where the homeless gathered. She arranged with the Salvation Army to give tokens to the homeless for a free taco. She wanted to do more, but she would be flooded with homeless if she didn't limit the number of tokens available. She fed the poor. She made good choices, thinking of others; he hadn't. He made selfish choices, thinking only of himself.

"We are the choices we make," Bonnie always said.

Lonny lit a cigarette, paced around his yard and then went into his house.

It was quiet inside.

"Sweetie." He called out to her, but there was no answer. Maybe she was riding or taking a walk. She liked to do that.

Lonny had been pinned to the news the last couple of weeks. Ansel Andover and Bertram Wagner were among a bunch of old guys who got sick and died of a flu in New Jersey. There was going to be an investigation. He wondered what they were looking to find and if that might tie back to him.

Lonny plopped down in front of the television and turned it on. The narrator of a nature show said, "In 1896, a Swedish scientist told the world that burning coal would make the earth warmer. 1896."

That was a long time ago, Lonny thought.

"The majority of scientists knew that this was definitely true by the 1960s. By the summer of 1988, then the hottest on record, scientists were clamoring at the public to pay attention."

Lonny had always thought the end of the world would start after he was dead. But the end had been coming for his whole life and he had ignored it, denied it. According to this narrator, the end of the world had arrived.

"Changes in climate will not be responsible for our demise," the narrator continued. "And this new virus that is out of control will not do it either. Self-serving, unethical, corrupt, and greedy people will be to blame. They need only make a few bad choices."

Lonny angrily clicked off the television.

He got up from his lazy boy and poured himself a drink. He paused and listened. He thought he heard something. There it was again. A moan.

Lonny ran down the hallway into the main bedroom. Bonnie was spread half on and half off the bed. Her face was purple and her eyes were swollen shut. She gasped for air, but not for long. She passed out just as he took her hand. He patted her face.

"Bonnie," he near shrieked. "Come on Honey. Open those baby blues," but she didn't. "No. No."

Lonny ran for the phone, but he couldn't get any kind of connection to 911.

He searched for a pulse in her wrist, but couldn't find one. He lay her flat on the floor and tried breathing into Bonnie's mouth, but he didn't know what he was doing. He couldn't see her chest rise and fall. She wasn't getting any air.

He tried 911 again and got the same irritating noise. He tried to conjure anyone he could think of that might be able to help him. No one. It was a thirty-minute drive to anywhere. He knew she was dead and she'd only be deader in thirty minutes.

Lonny hadn't realized until that moment how very much he loved her.

Chapter 57 – *Alonzo***, Sunday, May 4, 2026**

Lonny sat on the top of the hill with his ghosts. Bonnie hadn't joined them yet. He thought that was because she knew he would be with her soon.

When she died, he couldn't get anyone on the phone, so he drove her body into town and found it in chaos. The funeral home was already overrun and couldn't give Bonnie the respect that she deserved.

He took her home. He washed her in the clawfoot tub that she loved and dressed her in something pretty and then he dug a hole in the ground under a tall elm tree that she loved. He was mostly okay as he wrapped her in a flowered bedsheet and sewed it closed. She didn't look like her. Bonnie's light and smile were gone from him.

He placed her body in the hole as gently as he could, threw in some wild flowers from his field, and covered her in dirt. He sang Amazing Grace. He had a nice voice and he knew most of the words, at least for the first verse.

He felt sick. He'd had a fever off and on all day and he couldn't find his energy. He was confused and sluggish much of the time. He knew it wasn't just grief. He had kissed her right up until he lay her to rest. He had the J-flu like she had had. Dangerous. Deadly.

He'd heard all about it on the news as he drove to town and back. COVID-19 had been chaotic for a few years and over a million people died in the United States alone, but then things got better, especially for the Wagners and Andovers of the world—people who wanted to keep the world for themselves.

Lonny had finally figured it out. He had been a cog in a

chain of corruption that had killed his Bonnie, had killed him, and had killed so many more. If only, he had said 'no.' If only all the greedy cogs had said 'no.'

Lonny gasped for air. He couldn't get enough into his lungs. Still, it seemed a good idea to light up his cigarette. One drag and he fell into a coughing fit. His hand dropped to the ground which ignited the chemicals saturated within the earth and created a pillar of red, orange and gold. Beautiful. Bonnie had come for him.

Epilogue – *Mira and Miles* - Five Years Later

What had been beautiful lawns and lush gardens were turning brittle and brown-spotted despite any amount of watering that they managed to do. Mira and Miles had become the leaders of the forty or so people that lived in the hive. Everyone looked to them to figure out how to survive.

It wasn't raining. They barely got five inches a year now. Their stored drinking water was being rationed and the rain tower wasn't making more.

Miles decided to dig a well. He picked a greenish spot near the river where he hoped there was an underground flow. He hit water at ten feet, but he wanted to make the well as deep as possible to limit surface contamination. He used excavation equipment to get another twenty feet down. He created a five-foot shaft cribbed with dead trees and stones. It was arduous work to take containers to the well, fill them, get them back to the hive, and then boil it all, but that's what they had to do.

Many of the people in the hive moved back to Austin were there was still some water coming out of taps. This water was being highly rationed, but still, that was so much easier.

Geri and Tula were two among the couple dozen who moved back to Austin. They became a part of a group there that was teaching the unskilled generation, for that's what they fondly called the people too young to have any real survival skills when the world started to fall apart. Both Geri and Tula were extremely experienced in gardening. That was the focus of their contribution to the group.

Mira found herself pretty much among the unskilled, however she almost had a law degree. She decided to design a governance structure that was as fair and equitable as she could make it. There were very few laws, most having to do with killing, hurting or stealing.

Other kinds of rules went by the way-side. Mira and Miles were together. They loved each other and their two babies. They didn't need to be married to know that. Mira could see it in Miles eyes every morning when she wrapped her arms around him and kissed him. Miles knew it when he watched her read stories to the kids at nighttime.

"You should become one of the teachers when the kids are old enough to go to school," Miles said.

Mira smiled, "I've been thinking that myself." As it turned out, most of the people who stayed were the ones with children. A school-aged baby boom was beginning. "They'll need more teachers."

"Over by the fence, near the garden, there is a kinda green spot. I think I'll try to dig another well there."

"I love that idea." Mira said.

And they kissed for a long time, even though it was the middle of the day.

The End

About the Author

Nancy Smith is a writer of novels, novellas, screenplays and short stories. She is also a filmmaker, script analyst, and script supervisor. Nancy is the owner of First Look Script Analysis, operating since December 2005 and First Look Publishing operating since 2016. She lives in Austin, Texas.

For more information, please see:
http://www.nancysmithwriter.com

Books in this Series

This trilogy, called *After Normal*, takes place in a period from the year 2003 to 2045. When I started writing these books they were near future science fiction, but the world quickly caught up. The books describe a world crumbling to ruin.

Book One: *The Universal Vaccine*

A University of Texas at Austin art student comes home to find police on her doorstep. They tell her that her microbiologist mother and engineer father as well as all of her parents' coworkers are dead. Isa wants to understand what happened. She enlists the assistance of an investigative journalist to find out. The pair have no idea where this search will take them.

Book Two: *The Firebrand River*

Every weekend, there's a volleyball party by the Firebrand River until the weekend that strange, green pollution and a mysterious human finger bone shuts down the fun. The owner of the land works with police and an EPA investigator to help solve both an old mystery and a twenty-year old missing persons case.

Book Three: *The Slow Kill*

In the aftermath of a world ravaged by disease, fire, famine and drought, a botanist erects a biodome over Austin's Lake Travis in order to deter evaporation and protect his hydrofarm. However, plans to electrify and seal the dome's exterior, separate the haves from the have nots and force a desperate father apart from his wife and six-year-old son.

Other books/ebooks by Nancy Smith

Tainted Harvest

This book focuses on the experiences of Tituba, a slave sold in Barbados to Samuel Parris who would eventually become minister in Salem, MA. The book covers her life from the time of her enslavement through the 1692 witch trials. Tituba was the first person to confess to witchcraft. She told a tale at her hearing unlike anything that the Puritans had heard before, a story drawn from her own experiences and spiritual beliefs.

This novel is primarily based on the concepts presented by two noted academics. Linna Caporael went to the top of her class in 1976 when she made the connection between ergot poisoning on the rye during the 1692 growing season in Salam Village and the witch trials. Elaine Breslaw's 1996 book postulated that a clash of cultures between South American native, Tituba, and the New England Puritans added fuel to the fire.

<u>Novellas:</u>

Never Past (Mystery)

Kat Richardson was an ordinary woman, just like you, your mother or your grandmother, until someone chose to make her a victim. Who murdered this sixty-five-year-old retired teacher as she slept alone in her bed—despite the fact that she was secured behind a hard-core bedroom door with a heavy deadbolt. Detective Hedy Werth and her partner, Merton Manes, search for answers.

Picture Postcards (Romantic Drama Novella)

How can Virginia Mae Beauvoir learn to love when the people she most cares about in her life keep abandoning her? What she needs is a good teacher.

Stories Across Time (Short Story Collection)

This collection touches on the human moments of a variety people. The stories are placed in time anywhere within the last ten decades. It's up to the reader to intuit when that might be or if it even matters.

Book Excerpt: *The Slow Kill*

Chapter 1

June 2035

Hot. Scorching hot.

The weather forecaster blamed another unmoving high-pressure system for creating the relentless heat that daily shrouded them in triple-digit temperatures.

Frank Harvey ran. He hated jogging, but it settled his mind and loosened his muscles. He found his pace. His old cross-trainers, held together by layers of duct tape, slapped the path as Old Sol beat down on his shoulders. The sun had barely peeked over the horizon and he was sweating, but not as much as he would have thought. There was no moisture in the air. There was no moisture in him.

Frank zigzagged a dirty path lined with the dried and broken limbs of hackberry trees. The leaves left on the trees had turned brown before reaching maturity making it appear as if there had been a sudden, late cold snap, but there hadn't.

Frank sprinted down a natural culvert and around a rocky hillside. The dirt pit that was Lake Travis came into view.

Back in the 1940's, men had constructed a dam to create a reservoir on the Colorado River. The primary purpose of the reservoir called Lake Travis and several other linked reservoirs was to control flooding for the dramatically shifting water levels in the river. Water was managed, making it available for over a million people to drink. Lake Travis had been a large lake, often too vast to see from one side to the other. When full, Lake Travis held somewhere around 680 feet of water.

Frank pictured the lake as it had been in years past with

swimmers, fisherman and boaters of all kinds, from large pleasure crafts to paddle-boarders. Way back when, Frank hadn't been any of those things, not really. He liked to swim laps in the indoor pool at the University of Texas and he rowed crew on the long, straight stretch of the river. However, he did like to sit lakeside at a restaurant and drink Margaritas at sunset. He missed the yellows, purples and blues bouncing off clouds.

But Lake Travis was no longer full of water. It was no longer a lake. It looked as if a monster, too large to see from anywhere but space, had beaten a hole into the ground. A hundred foot of border lined the cracked earth in the middle of a dry basin.

At one time, islands and trees poked their heads out of the lake, but with no water the hills had been revealed and the trees had turned to pulp. Now, all that was had been bulldozed flat—a barren wasteland of dust that was free of all debris. The character of the lake was pushed into piles at the land end of long unused boat ramps.

Frank looked at one such pile. It contained boulder-size rocks, root balls from trees, a broken picnic table and bones from fish and animals. He examined one set of bones more closely. Was that a human femur? He wouldn't be surprised.

A glass and metal structure about fifty-acres square stood on the far side of the barren bed. Frank jogged toward it, his feet leaving prints in plumbs of dust.

He passed more boat docks that had caved into the ground, stranded on the parched, broken dirt. Boat debris littered the powdered earth nearby.

All except for one houseboat. It sat in dry dock on a tall scaffold made of freshly sawn lumber. The boat was a hundred-footer with a wood covered swimming platform at the front as well as a structure to hold a canvas top over the second story sun deck. The houseboat was mostly intact but in serious need of major repair.

Frank had bought the boat for practically nothing from a man who believed that Austin was a permanent desert and, if things continued on their current trajectory, would become even more desolate and infertile.

Frank climbed out of the lake pit at a boat dock. A pier ran into the center of the lake. The pier was long and tall, taller than the lake if it were full. He stood on the pier, now level with his boat on the scaffold. He ran his hand gently, lovingly over the gray wood of the hull and imagined it refurbished, polished and gleaming. In his mind's eye, he could see it bobbing on a full lake surrounded by a verdant shoreline.

An enormous cylinder, a pipe seeming to go nowhere, stretched into the lakebed and stopped at a pumping station near the middle. If viewed from space, its size belied, he might think the pipe was any sewer line. But, just like the Alaskan pipeline was built to deal with the 1973 oil crisis, this pipeline was built to deal with this current water crisis.

Above the edge of the dirt pit that had been the lake floor, construction was near completion on Frank's baby, an enormous hydro-farm, a long arched greenhouse, set high on concrete pilings that were solidly encased in glass and wire mesh making a 360-degree window around the farm.

One hundred feet from the farm was a dilapidated, broken power station shorn up by solar power from a home panel grid. Before the drought, many individuals had installed solar panels on the roofs of their homes and had sold any excess back to the city. At the time, the amount of electricity that the power station produced had been woefully inadequate causing black outs and shut downs. The solar power generated by the home panels had been swept up and targeted to the local hospitals and police stations with the promise that if there were excess it would be rationed back to the homes. He was still waiting for that to happen.

An assistant, Frank couldn't recall his name, a young man in dirty jeans, his thin hair pulled into a ratty ponytail, exited the building and grinned as he walked past Frank.

"Morning, Dr. Harvey."

"Hi there." Frank could tell by Pony's face that he knew that Frank didn't know his name. Frank had a dozen assistants, all of which he hired because they worked well independently. This allowed Frank to focus on what he needed to do.

"Big day," Pony said.

Frank nodded in acknowledgement. It was a big day. His heartbeat raced and not from his jog. Frank rested his hands on his knees, as he gasped for breath.

At the start of the famine, farmers had cut down their drought-ruined crops. With no hope of germination of the next crop, they hadn't bothered to plant more. With no water for the animals or their pasturelands, ranchers had sent their herds to market early. They'd auctioned beef and pork at triple price, until there was no more. The farmers had plowed under their last field and the ranchers had sold their last cow to market, thus guaranteeing a famine that could not end.

As dry as it was here, that's how wet it was on the east coast. Florida over to the Louisiana Gulf Coast overflowed with water, rivers of water, floods of water, water with nowhere to go.

Frank was determined to transport the water from where they had too much to the empty reservoir. There was no understating what a full lake could mean to the city. Austin could be one of the last places on earth where sunshine and water came together in reasonable proportions to make food.

Frank had gone to his boss, Pierce Wagner, with his idea for a pipeline. Frank worked for a think tank funded by the pharmaceutical manufacturer called the Wagner Company. The think tank looked for solutions to an ever-growing list of survival issues. The company was into everything.

Frank had done a lot of research into hydraulics, irrigation and water management. He had a plan for growing food, a good plan, one he knew would work.

"Aren't you a botanist? Wouldn't you need an engineer for

this?" Wagner had asked.

"I'll hire if I can. I'll figure it out if I can't."

"Hasn't a pipeline been tried before?"

"It failed for political reasons, not scientific ones."

"When was that? Before the collapse?"

Frank nodded.

Frank had been stunned when the Wagner Company funded his project instantly and completely. Pierce Wagner had practically thrown money at him.

Pushed by an ambitious schedule, Frank had built his pipeline from a water restoration and reclamation plant on the Mississippi River at Shreveport, Louisiana all the way to the refurbished water storage reservoir at the Lake Travis pumping station.

Shreveport was the most populated city within eight hundred miles. It lay about 335 miles east of Austin, across a vast expanse of parched nothing. Stragglers from what should have been upstream states including Arkansas, Oklahoma, Kansas, Missouri, Nebraska and Illinois poured into Shreveport from spaces where the ground was so sterilized that nothing would ever grow again. On the coast, the water level rose in Houston, Baton Rouge and New Orleans making those places inhospitable and so their populations escaped to Shreveport as well.

Shreveport had plenty of water and a good amount of sunshine, but food was pathetically insufficient to feed their ever-growing population. Shreveport had taken up arms to deter any further population increase, but they still needed additional resources from somewhere. He had heard a rumor that thousands of people had barricaded themselves in a casino — already a small village of its own — and protected themselves with whatever force was necessary.

Frank entered the back door of the glass hydroponics farm. Under a filtered glass skylight, row after row of dirt sat in what would soon be a mineral nutrient bath connected by a weave of intertwined gutters. Frank walked down an aisle, checking on pictures, signs that indicated what would sprout with regular water: strawberry vines, tomatoes and green beans.

Hundreds of thousands had died in Austin alone. Billions had died around the world. They died from disease and then starvation. This was his responsibility, his job—to create food—to save them all.

www.ingramcontent.com/pod-product-compliance
Lightning Source LLC
Chambersburg PA
CBHW051520150726
47997CB00001B/320